A MAN ... HIS WORLD ... HIS WOMEN

Benjamin: He searched for a point of balance in a life filled with momentary passions, well-mixed martinis and inescapable memories ...

Peggy: Intelligent, devoted, loving, she was the perfect wife—giving him everything he could want, except his freedom ...

Leah: She was a beautiful mistress—and too voluptuous a woman for a married man to forget ...

"A questing hero, wartime vignettes, sex that foregoes the leer for the lyric—Irwin Shaw's VOICES OF A SUMMER DAY is a very good novel ... perhaps his best ... a moving portrait that brilliantly reflects the turmoils and triumphs of contemporary man."
—*National Observer*

Books by Irwin Shaw

NOVELS

* *Voices of a Summer Day*
* *The Young Lions*
* *The Troubled Air*
* *Lucy Crown*
* *Two Weeks in Another Town*
* *Rich Man, Poor Man*
* *Evening in Byzantium*
* *Nightwork*
* *Beggarman, Thief*
* *The Top of the Hill*

SHORT STORY COLLECTIONS

Sailor off the Bremen
Welcome to the City
Act of Faith
Mixed Company
Tip on a Dead Jockey
* *Love on a Dark Street*
* *God Was Here, but He Left Early*

PLAYS

Bury the Dead
The Gentle People
Sons and Soldiers
The Assassin
Children from Their Games

NONFICTION

In the Company of Dolphins
* *Paris! Paris!*

* Available in Dell Editions

IRWIN SHAW

VOICES OF A SUMMER DAY

LAUREL

A LAUREL BOOK
Published by
DELL PUBLISHING CO., INC.
1 Dag Hammarskjold Plaza
New York, N.Y. 10017

Laurel ® TM 674623, Dell Publishing Co., Inc.

ISBN: 0-440-39335-3

Reprinted by arrangement with Delacorte Press
Printed in the United States of America
Previous Dell Edition #9355
Two previous Dell editions
First Laurel printing—September 1984

VOICES OF A
SUMMER DAY

THE RED FLAG WAS UP WHEN HE DROVE UP TO THE house. He went in. The house was silent. "Peggy," he called. "Peggy!" There was no answer. His wife was not there nor either of his children.

He went out and looked at the ocean. The waves were ten feet high and there was about eight hundred yards of foam ripping between the tide line, marked by seaweed, and the whitecaps of the open Atlantic. The beach was deserted except for a tall girl in a black bathing suit, who was walking along the water's edge with two Siamese cats pacing beside her. The girl had long blond hair that hung down her back and blew in the wind. Her legs and arms were pollen-colored against the sea, and the cats made a small pale jungle at her ankles. The girl was too far away for him to tell whether she was pretty or not and she didn't look in his direction, but he wished he knew her. He wished he knew her well enough to call out and see her smile and wait for him to join her so that they could walk along the beach together, attended by toy tigers, the noise of the surf beating at them

7

as she told him why a girl like that walked alone
on an empty beach on a bright summer afternoon.

He watched her grow smaller and smaller in the
distance, the cats, the color of the desert, almost
disappearing against the sand. She was outlined for
a last moment against the dazzle of the waves and
then the beach was empty again.

It was no afternoon for swimming, and the girl
was gone, and he didn't feel like hanging around
the house alone so he went in and changed his
clothes and got into the car and drove into town.
On the high school field, there was a pickup game
of baseball in progress, boys and young men and
several elderly athletes who by Sunday morning
would regret having slid into second base on Saturday afternoon.

He saw his son playing center field. He stopped
the car and got out and lay back in the sun on the
hot planks of the benches along the third-base line,
a tall, easy-moving man with a powerful, graying
head. He was dressed in slacks and a short-sleeved
blue cotton shirt, the costume of a man consciously
on holiday. On the long irregular face there were
the not unexpected signs of drink and overwork.
He was no longer young, and, although at a distance his slimness and way of moving gave a decep-
tive appearance of youth, close-up age was there,
experience was there, above all around the eyes,
which were deep black, almost without reflections,
hooded by heavy lids and a dark line of thick lash-
es that suggested secret Mediterranean mourning
against the olive tint of the skin stretched tight

8

over jutting cheek bones. He greeted several of the players and spectators, and the impression of melancholy was erased momentarily by the good humor and open friendliness of his voice. The combination of voice and features was that of a man who might be resigned and often cynical, but rarely suspicious. He was a man who permitted himself to be cheated in small matters. Taxi drivers, employees, children, and women took advantage of him. He knew this, each time it happened, and promptly forgot it.

On the field, the batter was crouching and trying to work the pitcher for a walk. The batter was fifteen years old and small for his age. The pitcher was six feet three inches tall and had played for Columbia in 1947.

The third baseman, a boy of eighteen named Andy Roberts, called out, "Do you want to take my place, Mr. Federov? I promised I'd be home by four."

"Thanks, no, Andy," Federov said. "I batted 072 last season and I've hung up my spikes."

The boy laughed. "Maybe you'd have a better season this year if you tried."

"I doubt it," Federov said. "It's very rare that your average goes up after fifty."

The batter got his walk, and while he was throwing his bat away and trotting down to first base Federov waved to his son out in center field. His son waved back. "Andy," Federov said, "how's Mike doing?"

"Good field, no hit," Andy said.

"Runs in the family," said Federov. "My father never hit a curve ball in his life either."

The next batter sent a line drive out toward right center, and Michael made a nice running catch over his shoulder and pivoted and threw hard and accurately to first base, making the runner scramble back hurriedly to get there before the throw. Michael was left-handed and moved with that peculiar grace that left-handers always seemed to Federov to have in all sports. There had never been a left-hander before in Federov's family, nor in his wife's family that he knew of, and Federov sometimes wondered at this genetic variance and took it as a mark of distinction, a puzzling designation, though whether for good or ill he could not say. Michael's sister, eleven years old and too smart for her age, as Federov sometimes told her, teased Michael about it. "Sinister, sinister," she chanted when she disagreed with her brother's opinons, "Old Pope Sinister the First."

Old Pope Sinister the First popped up to short-stop his next time at bat and then came over to sit beside his father. "Hi, Dad." He touched his father lightly but affectionately on the shoulder. "How're things in the dirty city?"

"Dirty," Federov said. He and his brother ran a building and contracting business together, and while there was a lot of work unfinished on both their desks, the real reason the brothers had stayed in New York on a hot Saturday morning was to try to arrange a settlement with Louis's third wife, whom he wanted to divorce to marry a fourth wife, and who was all for a vengeful and scandalous action in court. Louis was the architect of the firm, and this connection with the arts, plus his quiet good looks, made him a prey for women and a permanent subsidy for the legal profession.

"Where's your mother?" Federov asked his son. "The house was empty when I got in."

"Bridge, hairdresser's, I don't know," Michael said carelessly. "You know—dames. She'll turn up for dinner."

"I'm quite sure she will," Federov said.

Michael's side was retired, and he picked up his glove and started toward his position in the field. "Mike," Federov said, "you swung at a high ball, you know."

"I know," Michael said. "I'm a confirmed sinner."

He was thirteen years old but, like his sister, was a ransacker of libraries and often sounded it.

Five minutes later there was a dispute about a close call at first base, and two or three boys shouted, good-naturedly, "Oh, you bum!" and "Kill the umpire!"

"Stop that!" Federov said sharply. Then he was as surprised as the boys themselves by the harshness of his tone. They kept quiet after that, although they eyed him curiously. Ostentatiously, Federov looked away from them. He had heard the cry thousands of times before, just as the boys had, and he didn't want to have to explain what was behind his sudden explosion of temper. Ever since the President had been shot, Federov, sometimes consciously, sometimes unconsciously, had refrained from using words like "kill" or "murder" or "shoot" or "gun," and had skipped them, when he could, in the things he read, and moved away from conversations in which the words were likely to come up. He had heard about the mocking black-bordered advertisement in the Dallas newspaper that had greeted the President on his arrival in the city, and he had read about the minister who said that schoolchildren in the city had cheered upon being told of the President's death, and he had heard from a lineman friend of his on the New York Giants football team that, after the game they had played in Dallas ten days after the President was killed, an open car full of high school boys and girls had followed the Giants' bus through downtown Dallas, chanting, "Kennedy gawn, Johnson next, Kennedy gawn, Johnson next."

"Kids," the lineman had said wonderingly, "just kids, like anybody else's kids. You couldn't believe it. And nobody tried to stop them."

Kids, just kids. Like the boys on the field in front of him. Like his own son. In the same blue jeans, going to the same kind of schools, listening to the same awful music on radio and television, playing the same traditional games, loved by their parents as he loved his son and daughter. Kids shouting a tribal chant of hatred for a dead man who had been better than any of them could ever hope to be.

The hell with it, he thought. You can't keep thinking about it forever.

With an effort of will he made himself fall back into lazy afternoon thoughtlessness. Soon, lulled by the slow familiar rhythm of the game, he was watching the field through half-dozing, sun-warmed eyes, lying back and not keeping track of what was happening as boys ran from base to base, stopped grounders, changed sides. He saw his son make two good plays and one mediocre one without pride or anxiety. Michael was tall for his age, and broad, and Federov took what he realized was a normal fatherly pleasure in watching his son's movements as, loose-limbed and browned by the sun, he performed in the wide green spaces of the outfield.

Dozing, almost alone on the rows of benches, one game slid into other games, other generations were at play many years before . . . in Harrison, New Jersey, where he had grown up; on college campuses, where he had never been quite good enough to make the varsity, despite his fleetness of foot and sure-handedness in the field. The sounds were the same through the years—the American sounds of summer, the tap of bat against ball, the cries of the infielders, the wooden plump of the ball into catchers' mitts, the umpires calling "Strike three and you're out." The generations circled the bases, the dust rose for forty years as runners slid in from third, dead boys hit doubles, famous men made errors at shortstop, forgotten friends tapped the clay from their spikes with their bats as they stepped into the batter's box, coaches' voices warned, across the decades, "Tag up, tag up!" on fly balls. The distant, mortal innings of boyhood and youth . . .

—————————— 1927 ——————————

BENJAMIN FEDEROV HELD HIS BROTHER LOUIS'S HAND. They had both been to the camp the year before, but Benjamin's parents had made a last plea to him to take good care of Louis, who was only nine.

The camp was in Vermont and was reached from New York by a night voyage on the Fall River Line and buses for the rest of the way. On the evening of June 30, 1927, long before sailing time, the shed at the foot of Fulton Street began to fill with boys and parents and the counselors who were doomed for two months to protect everybody's little darling from drowning, snakebite, homesickness, and moral contamination. Here and there a small boy wept because he was being taken away from his parents for the first time, but the atmosphere in the old dark shed, smelling from salt and years of odorous cargo, was chaotically festive, as mothers kissed children good-bye and fathers

14

sought out counselors to tell them that their sons wet their beds or walked in their sleep or had to be prevented from diving because of sinus trouble. Whistles blew, lost tennis racquets were discovered at the last moment, and the holiday began in an excited straggle up the gangplank.

Trying to appear sophisticated, Benjamin waited for most of the other boys to go aboard before starting up with Louis's hand in his. Even then, the difference between the two brothers was already marked. Benjamin was tall and large for his age, with an athlete's muscles and movements and an impatient physical and mental quickness. Louis, with a cherubic high brow and curling golden hair, was quiet, dreamy, inward, neither social nor antisocial, reserved in his affections, non-assertive, and beneath it all, unmovably stubborn. Surprisingly, he was a ferocious fighter when challenged and had consistently beaten boys two or three years older than he on the block in Harrison on which the Federovs lived.

Israel Federov, Louis and Benjamin's father, had come from Russia at the age of six, one of a family that eventually numbered eight children. He had grown up amongst the usual terrors and sweated labor on New York's East Side and only in the nineteen twenties had begun to prosper in a small automobile-accessory business that he and a partner ran on the outskirts of Newark. The fact that now, in 1927, he could afford to spend six hundred dollars to give his two sons a summer in the mountains seemed in the nature of a miracle to him. Even earlier, the realization of the immense difference of what his life would have been like if his family had remained in Russia instead of immigrating to America, had made him the most blindly ardent of patriots. Despite the fact that he was married and had one child, with another on the way, he had enlisted in 1917, leaving Benjamin's mother to scrape along on what she could earn as a piano teacher and on what her own family, who were almost equally poor, could spare for her in her husband's absence.

Israel was so committed to what he thought was his plain duty to the country that had taken him in that he had had one of his rare quarrels with his family on the subject. He had a younger brother, Samuel, aged twenty, who was studying to be a pianist and who regarded Chopin and Schumann as more important than any war. At a family conference it was decided that one crazy brother going to fight a war was enough for one family and that Samuel, following a custom consecrated by tradition for centuries in the Jewish villages of Russia, would have himself deliberately ruptured (there were experts at this among all the immigrant communities) and thus be unfit for military service. Cutting off a finger, another sensible device for avoiding the recruiting sergeant in Russia, was considered and rejected as being unrealistic for a pianist. Israel had stormed out of the house, saying he would never speak to any of them again if Samuel went through with the proposal.

Awed by his brother's rage, Samuel had dutifully reported to his draft board, only to be told, to his great relief, that he had a heart murmur, and was rejected. He played the piano happily from then on, although it was years before Israel finally forgave him.

His quick and spontaneous enlistment in the Army of the United States fighting a war that Israel would never admit, to the end of his days, was bungled, unnecessary and disastrous in its consequences, was the one purely selfish act that Israel Federov ever committed in all the seventy-one years of his lifetime.

The funnel horn blew, the ropes were cast off, the last handkerchief waved on the pier, and the boys lined the rail watching the buildings of New York slide by in the splendid mild evening light as the ship steamed up the river toward Long Island Sound and the calm open sea beyond Montauk.

Benjamin went down to his stateroom before they reached Hell Gate Bridge. He had bought a new fielder's glove two Saturdays before, having made the long trip from Harrison to a shop on Nassau Street in downtown New York that had a reputation for baseball equipment. The glove was an Eddie Roush model and had cost five dollars and fifty cents. Benjamin was very serious about baseball. He hadn't trusted putting the glove in the foot locker that had been sent off with all the camp uniforms and sweaters and socks with name tapes sewed on by his mother. He took the glove out of his overnight bag and a bottle of neat's-foot oil, which was the only oil to break a glove in with, and sat on his bunk in the stateroom, rubbing the oil into the new leather and pounding his fist into the glove to make a secure pocket, as the white ship throbbed steadily and the salt breeze, with its promise of future, incalculable voyages, swept in through the open porthole. There was a possiblity, which he recognized later on, that this was the happiest moment of his life, and he regretted it when a counselor opened the door to his cabin and told him that it was time to go to dinner.

They reached the camp in buses late the next afternoon and, after they had thrown their belongings on their cots in the six-man tents in which they were to live for two months and had dutifully taken the spoonful of castor oil that officially opened the camp season, all the older boys stripped and ran out onto the large grass square around which the tents were grouped. They wore spikes and baseball caps and carried their gloves, but aside from that they were naked as they shagged flies that two counselors fungoed out to them from the end of the square. The mountain air was cool, the lake three hundred yards away glittered in the light of the descending sun, the winter-white, quick bodies flashed across the coarse grass in an unembarrassed and joyous rite that cleansed forty boys of ten months of decorum, school, constricting clothing, the tabus of the grown-up world. The long summer of adolescence was before them, with its games, its mountains, its smells of balsam and blossoms and lake water, its competitions and lib-

18

erated laughter, and they saluted the young season in primal nakedness as they raced across the turf and leaped, in a flashing clatter of spiked shoes, to steal catches from each other. Illness and age were impossible then, for an hour or two, and even September was an eon in the future on that first afternoon of July, 1927.

Because Benjamin was so large and could more than hold his own in sports with older boys, he was put in a tent of seniors, all of them between fifteen and seventeen. During the day the difference in age didn't count particularly, but after taps, when all lights were out and the other boys began to talk about such things as cigarettes, liquor and girls, he lay quietly on his cot, looking up at the stars through the open sides of the tent, feeling childish and uninitiated. He had read much more than any of the other boys, but it was one thing to have thumbed through Mlle de Maupin behind the locked door of his room while pretending to be doing his homework and quite another to lie in the fragrant dark and listen to a sixteen-year-old boy describe how he had seduced a virgin in Lakewood, New Jersey, the summer before. "I took her cherry under a cherry tree," the boy said, and then went on with a detailed account of the performance that left Benjamin shaken and full of a trembling longing that he was sure would never be satisfied in his lifetime.

He had never kissed a girl (he was convinced he wasn't good-looking enough for this ever to happen to him), he had never smoked a cigarette (he wanted to be an All-American halfback), and never drunk a drop of alcohol (at the age of thirteen he doubted that he would be welcome in a speakeasy). He was by nature truthful and could not boast, like the other boys, who, while not going as far as the cherry-tree boy, spoke knowingly of kissing with open mouths, putting their hands under girls' skirts and getting drunk on their parents' hidden liquor on holidays.

The cherry-tree boy was named Boris Cohn. About two-thirds of the campers were Jewish. Somehow, in 1927, this easy association of Jew with Christian seemed natural and unforced. Only after the advent of Hitler would a similar mixture bear the burden of self-consciousness. Cohn came from a wealthy family in Manhattan, which had obviously spared no expense to spoil him. He had arrived in camp with a portable phonograph and a large collection of popular records. He went often to the theatre, he said, especially to musical comedies, took girls to restaurants, visited whorehouses, drank bathtub gin, smoked secretly, and insisted that he had driven a Packard phaeton for two weeks the summer before in Lakewood, New Jersey, using an older brother's license and getting away with it. To put the seal on his exalted status, he had brought with him two dozen new Spalding tennis balls. Benjamin, like his other tent-mates, had brought a box of three balls, which he knew would have to last him the summer.

The phonograph blared for hours each day.

Cohn had a particular liking for two songs, "Halle-lujah" and "Sometimes I'm Happy," from a musi-cal comedy called *Hit the Deck*. Cohn would play them over and over again, practicing dance steps barefooted on the rough plank floor of the tent. The terrible thing about Cohn from Benjamin's point of view was that, despite his depravity, he was generous and good-natured and was the best athlete in camp. He was the trickiest pitcher, with a curve, a drop, and a floater, he was the fastest runner in the 100- and 220-yard dash, he led the entire camp league in batting, he won the tennis tournament for seniors, he knocked out his oppo-nent in the first round of the 150-pound finals, he beat the next man by five yards in the 100-yard free-style and won the mile swim across the lake by nearly 300 yards. He also dispensed largesse to whoever happened to be present upon the arrival of the luxurious packages his parents sent him two or three times a week. Two hours after mail call he never had as much as a Hershey bar left for him-self. He also masturbated serenely when there were no counselors present. At the age of thirteen Cohn managed to shake, for life, Benjamin's sense of morality and his belief in the rewards of virtue and the wisdom of his elders.

The counselor for the tent, a darkly handsome, thick young man by the name of Bryant, who was a second-string halfback for Syracuse, was completely under Cohn's spell and didn't even report Cohn when he caught Cohn smoking one night after

21

taps. Bryant suffered from two obsessions. One was that he was going to be bald by the time he was twenty-five (which, in the event, turned out to be optimistic, as he was bald by his twenty-fourth birthday). The other was that he was better than the first-string Syracuse halfback and was only kept on the bench by an irrational dislike that the coach of the team had taken for him. Of all the five boys in the tent, Bryant discussed these weighty matters only with Cohn, who promised to find him the name of a doctor who had saved Cohn's uncle's hair under similar circumstances. Cohn also loaned Bryant a jar of expensive hair cream and, on two occasions, on Bryant's day off, a ten-dollar bill. He also promised that another uncle of his, who was a graduate of Syracuse and a weighty influence in alumni affairs, would personally talk to the coach in Bryant's behalf. Rich in everything, Cohn had an uncle for all eventualities. Actually, the next season, poor Bryant was demoted to third string and never even won his letter, but there was no way for him to know about his impending tragedy as he conferred in low tones throughout the summer with the all-powerful Cohn.

To the tune of "Sing Hallelujah, Hallelujah, sweep all your troubles away . . ." and "Sometimes I'm happy, sometimes I'm blue, My disposition depends on you . . . ," the summer passed, swinging into August on a chant of exultant optimism or Broadway melancholy, as the mood seized Cohn, cranking the handle of his phonograph and dancing barefoot on the tent floor.

1964

I TOOK HER CHERRY UNDER A CHERRY TREE, FEDEROV remembered nearly forty years later, *her, cherry, cherry, cherry, under the cherry, cherry tree*. Old English ballad.

There was a shout of warning and Federov looked up just in time to see a foul ball coming at him. He could have stood up and cupped the ball safely in his two hands or let it go entirely, but instead, at the last moment, he stretched debonairly above his head and caught the ball with his left hand. The boys on the field laughed and there were a few cheers for the catch, and Federov made a grave baseball player's salute, as though he were doffing his cap to an admiring crowd, before he tossed the ball to the pitcher. The ball had stung his palm and had broken a nail and his finger was bleeding a little, but he put his hand into his pocket and dried the blood off against the cloth. It would have been more sanitary to wrap a handkerchief around his finger, but he didn't want to let on that the catch had been more troublesome than it had seemed. Showboat, he thought. Two hands for beginners. He smiled wryly at the everlasting vanity of old athletes.

OTHER THINGS HAPPENED TO BENJAMIN THAT SUM-
mer. He played in three games on the senior varsity and made a diving catch in center field to save a
victory against another camp that brought him the
election of the Best Athlete of the Week at the Friday night ceremony of awards. Cohn gave him five
dollars for the catch, because Cohn was pitching at
the time. Benjamin didn't get paid again for en-
gaging in any sport until he played two or three
games of semipro football in Newark for twenty-
five dollars an afternoon the year after he got out of
college, during the Depression.

And for the first time in his life, that summer he
shed tears for someone besides himself. That long
step toward maturity came after the finals of the
boxing tournament, in which his brother Louis
was beaten in three rounds for the seventy-five-
pound championship by a boy two years older than
he. At the end of the fight, Louis's lip was cut and
there was a big lump on his forehead. Louis took
his beating with his usual stoicism, but, while Benjamin was leading him to the showers to stop the

flow of blood and put an icy washrag against Louis's forehead, the tears of helpless love suddenly came to Benjamin's eyes. He turned his head, trying to keep Louis from seeing what was happening. But he knew that Louis knew, though they never talked about the moment, even when they were grown men. Louis looked at him gravely, wondering and a little ashamed of what seemed to him incomprehensible childishness in a brother he had never seen weep before.

Each summer, toward the end of the camp season, the seniors went on a three-day trip, usually to play baseball and basketball against other camps within a radius of 200 miles or so. But this summer Cohn had to be reckoned with. After supper one night on the lawn outside the mess hall, in a general meeting of the seniors that he had persuaded the head counselor to call, Cohn stood up, smiling and at ease, as usual, and made a speech. "I got a great idea, fellers," he said. "Let's be different for once. We've been playing ball all season long. What's the sense in driving all over the place in trucks just to play some more ball? Anyway, we're more than forty of us and only about fifteen fellars're going to play, while all the rest of the guys just sit around like dopes. I don't think that's fair. After all, everybody's paying the same twenty bucks extra for the trip, why should only fifteen guys have all the fun?" There were some cheers at this unusual example of self-sacrifice, since everybody knew that Cohn would pitch both days and play in both basketball games. Benjamin listened with sinking heart. He covered center field for the varsity and had dreamed of batting against pitchers he had never seen before and stealing base hits from strange hitters for the glory of his team. Summer meant baseball for him. If it weren't for baseball, Benjamin wouldn't have cared if it was winter all year round.

He watched Cohn's persuasive brown monkey face as Cohn spoke and knew that something precious, something that in justice really belonged to him, was being taken away from him because of the strength of someone else's character and the cleverness of somebody else's mind. Somehow, he knew, too, that this was not the last time this would happen to him. He couldn't hate Cohn for it. You couldn't hate Cohn. Nobody could hate Cohn. You could only recognize his power.

"I happened to call an uncle of mine in Boston yesterday," Cohn said. Again that all-conquering phalanx of uncles. "And my uncle said, 'I'd like to give the boys a treat.' I don't know whether you boys know it or not," Cohn went on, "but a lot of times Broadway shows play in Boston before they come to New York. My uncle says there's a musical comedy in Boston now called *Bye, Bye Bonnie* that's just a wow. Comedians, chorus girls, the whole thing. My uncle says it'll cost a fortune to see it when it gets to New York, but he knows the man who owns the theatre and he's getting us all the best seats in the house next Tuesday . . ." A loud cheer went up from the listening boys. Cohn

grinned, before silencing them with a wave of the
hand. "And that ain't all. The night after, he's
going to give us a party. A real party." Cohn
winked lewdly. "If you know what I mean. Fancy
food, lobster, baked Alaska, punch . . . If there
weren't any of our good old couselors here, I'd tell
you what there's going to be in that little old
punch. Not just fruit juice, if you catch what I
mean, not in *my* uncle's house." Everybody laughed
at this, including Bryant and the other senior
counselor present. "And that ain't all, either. My
uncle has two daughters." He paused skillfully to
let this sink in. "Beauts. And I'm not saying this
just because they're my cousins. And not kids. Old.
Fifteen, seventeen, that sort of thing. And they've
been around. Don't let anybody tell you Boston is
a dead town. I was there last Christmas and they
practically had to carry me to the train. And these
girls ain't alone, fellers. They know everybody.
But *everybody*. Blonds, brunettes, girls from Vassar, Radcliffe. *College* girls. And they're all on notice, just sitting there waiting for us to say, 'Lady,
may I have the next dance?' " Now Cohn was saluted by whistles. He stopped the demonstration with
another easy, masterful wave of a hand. "And if
there's anybody who just can't get along without
baseball, why the Braves're playing Chicago while
we're there and my uncle'll get whoever wants to
go box seats, the best seats in the park. Now if this
ain't more fun than eating hamburgers and drinking cocoa and playing on a field at Camp Canoga
that's no smoother than a cow pasture and where

you ought to wear a catcher's mask in the outfield to protect yourself from the bad hops, I'll eat Benny Federov's five-dollar-and-fifty-cent Eddie Roush glove."

Even Benjamin felt he had to smile, hypocritically, as the boys laughed at Cohn's offer. Benjamin's passion was well-known and had been the subject of jokes several times in the skits put on in the Social Hall every Saturday evening.

"Benny," Cohn said charmingly, "you're not going to be sore at me, are you? You know how much I admire you. I've been around a lot and I've seen a lot of ballplayers and I don't mind saying I never saw a more promising outfielder in my life. Why . . ." Cohn addressed the meeting at large again. "Why, when it's two out and I'm pitching, and the ball's hit out toward center field, I don't even look around, no matter where it's going. I just throw away my glove and start walking toward the bench because I know Benny's out there and if Benny's out there that ball's going to be caught." He took a few shrewd, defense-attorney's steps toward Benjamin. "You're not sore, are you, Benny?"

"No," Benjamin said, "I'm not sore." Sore was not the word for what he was feeling, anyway, and at the age of thirteen he didn't know the accurate word for what Cohn was doing to him, and there was a good chance he would never learn the accurate word or have it ready for the proper occasion any time in his life.

"Anyway," Cohn said, going back to his original

position facing the boys seated in front of him on the grass in front of the mess hall, "all this is just a suggestion. If you fellers don't want to go to Boston that's okay with me. I'll get in there and pitch like it was the World Series and I was Dazzy Vance. I'm just as happy one way or another. All I think is, maybe we ought to vote. This is a free country and the majority rules and all that bunk. *Bye, Bye, Bonnie* or Camp Canoga. It's up to you."

Bye, Bye, Bonnie went for forty-one votes, Camp Canoga for two, Benjamin's and that of a boy called Burke, who didn't even play on either of the teams, but who had a grandmother in Boston he'd have to lunch with if she found out he was in the city.

Cohn's uncle got the tickets for *Bye, Bye, Bonnie* for August 23rd. The plans had been made in advance and nobody had bothered to find out that on that same day, two men called Sacco and Vanzetti were to be executed in Charlestown State Prison. Few of the boys read anything but the sports pages of whatever newspapers found their way into the camp, but the director of the camp, who was the principal of a high school in the wintertime, read the front pages, too, and they were full of threats of riots, bombings, and mob action in Boston if the execution were carried out as scheduled.

The director had an understandable reluctance to send forty-three boys entrusted to his care into a city crammed, as the papers said, with violent anarchists from all over the world, and in which street fighting and bombings were likely to take place.

He called the seniors together and gave them a short course in contemporary history. When he told the boys that the Boston trip might have to be canceled, the boys responded with groans. "But it is not yet definite," the director went on. He was an impressive, calm-looking man with a priest's bald head and a fine tonsure of clipped white hair. But he was hounded all summer by fear for the tender souls turned trustingly over to him by parents every June 30th. "No, not definite at all," the director said. "There have been protests all over the world, there is a great deal of confusion in this case, and I wouldn't be surprised if at any moment the Governor of Massachusetts, who is a personal friend of mine, and a great and just man, either reprieved these poor men to wait for another investigation or commuted their sentences. We will have to wait for events," the director said, and it was probably the first time in their lives that any of the boys listening to him had ever heard that phrase. "We will make double arrangements, both with Camp Canoga and Camp Berkeley, and with the proper people in Boston, so that no matter what happens, you boys will not be deprived of your holiday. If the poor men are to die, you will still have your two baseball games and basketball games. If, even at the last minute, we hear that the men are to live, you will have your rather extraordinary . . . uh . . . spree, in Boston."

As the boys straggled disconsolately back to their

bunks, Benjamin found himself next to Cohn. "What's the matter, Cohn?" Benjamin asked. "Isn't the Governor one of your uncles?" It was the sharpest thing he had said in all his thirteen years, and Cohn looked at him, surprised, as the realization hit him that there were people on the face of the earth who might disapprove of him and whom he could not charm and who might be pleased to make him suffer.

On the morning of the 23rd, the forty-three boys and four counselors piled into Reo trucks with benches along the sides behind the driver's cab. The passengers were protected by canvas stretched over wooden supports, but the back was open. It was a raw, gusty day, and the boys all wore sweaters as they piled onto the wooden seats. The latest rumor from Boston was that the Governor had not yet made up his mind about whether to show clemency to the convicted men. Bryant, who was in charge of the expedition, was to call the camp director at one o'clock for final instructions. If by that time the execution had been postponed or canceled, the trucks were to continue on to Boston. If the men had been electrocuted, the trucks were to go on to Camp Canoga. The boys would play the baseball game, stay the night, and play the basketball game the next morning. Then they were to go on to Camp Berkeley, repeat the program and start back toward camp the following afternoon.

Two or three of the older boys had newspapers

with them and were making predictions that the Governor would have to commute the sentence. Benjamin, although an avid reader of everything else, had not yet begun to read newspapers and had no opinion of any kind on the rights and wrongs of the case and no notion of why such a fuss was being made about two men he had never heard of. Hundreds of people were electrocuted or hanged each year throughout the United States, he knew, without its interfering with anybody's plans and the special nature of this particular punishment eluded him.

He glanced at a newspaper column that compared it to the Dreyfus case, but since Benjamin had never heard of the Dreyfus case this was of no help to him.

He sat as close to the open back of the truck as he could get, bumping on the hard bench, smelling the dusty canvas top and hoping he wouldn't get carsick. He didn't join in the jokes but sat gloomily, with eyes closed, concentrating to keep from being nauseated by the fumes from the engine and the roughness of the trip. He did not actively wish for the death of Sacco and Vanzetti that day, but if he had been told definitely that the men were not to die, he would have begged out of the trip and stayed in camp. Boston had no attraction for him. He had no interest in the theatre; the spiked punch of Cohn's uncle would, he was sure, make him sick, and he had no illusions about the amount of attention the sixteen- and seventeen-

year-old blonds and brunettes from Vassar and
Radcliffe would lavish on him at a party. And in
camp he could always scrounge games in the Inter-
mediate League or take a couple of books in a canoe and catch up on his reading. So his presence in
the truck was in reality a bet that the men would
die and he would get a chance to play two ball
games in the next three days.

As the Reos rolled along the rough narrow roads
of 1927 New England, sending up clouds of white
dust between the stands of second-growth pine, the
boys in the truck with Benjamin began to sing.
Since Cohn was in the same truck, they naturally
sang "Hallelujah" and "Sometimes I'm happy,
sometimes I'm blue." Benjamin sat silent, not singing, hating the songs (in lieu of hating Cohn),
feeling his hair and clothes getting gritty from the
dust and conscious of a sour contraction in the pit
of his stomach. Many years later, as a sergeant in
the infantry, sitting by the tailgate of a weapons-
carrier full of men, rolling across the plains of
France after St. Lô, with a khaki handkerchief
across the lower part of his face to keep out the
dust, he had a curious feeling that he had done all
this before, had felt exactly the same during another summer, that soon adolescent, unarmed voices
on the road past Avranches would start chanting,
"Sing, Hallelujah—and you'll shoo the blues away;
when cares pursue you—Hallelujah—gets you
through the darkest day."

Cohn stood up between the two rows of benches,

keeping his balance easily as the truck swayed from side to side, conducting the choir, swinging his arms and making pained grimaces in imitation of an orchestra leader dissatisfied with the sounds his musicians were producing. The song ended in laughter at Cohn's clowning and he spread both his arms, still in mimicry, and said, "Rise, gentlemen, rise."

Everybody but Benjamin stood up. Even Bryant stood up with the others, going along with the joke. Cohn looked speculatively at Benjamin, and Benjamin was afraid Cohn was going to make a joke about him, but Cohn merely smiled, then began to improvise, first humming a little to himself as the boys sat down again, then going into his own words to the tune of "Sometimes I'm Happy."

"Sometimes I'm happy," Cohn sang, "sometimes I'm blue. Sacco, Vanzetti, what did you do? Dear Mr. Governor, can't you be fine, And turn the juice on some other time?"

Somehow, by humming or going fast over the rough spots, Cohn managed to make his words fit the beat of the music and he grinned at the shout of laughter that greeted his cleverness.

"Now," he said, "all together . . ."

"Sometimes I'm happy . . . ," the young voices sang over the noise of the motors. And, "Sacco, Vanzetti, what did you do?"

Only Benjamin sat silent. Everything's a joke to that sonofabitch, he thought bitterly, knowing that all the boys in the truck would call him a sorehead from then on and not caring.

"Dear Mr. Governor, can't you be fine, And turn the juice on some other time?"

The voices sang louder and louder as the boys learned the words, and they were bawling the song out when the trucks stopped at one o'clock in front of the post office and general store of a small village and Bryant went in to call the director of the camp.

The village green, with its bandstand, was in front of the general store, and all the boys got out and stretched their legs and sat on the grass or on the steps of the bandstand and ate the sandwiches and oranges and drank the manufactured-tasting milk from thermos jugs that had been sent along by the camp cooks with their lunches.

Bryant took a long time, and while waiting for him Cohn taught his new song to the boys from the other trucks. The village was almost deserted, since it was lunchtime, and there was only a farmer or two passing through to listen puzzledly to the strange sound of more than forty boys in camp uniforms singing, in voices that ranged from childish soprano to uncertain bass: "Sacco, Vanzetti, what did you do?"

When Bryant came out of the general store he had a ponderous, self-important look on his face, like the manager of a baseball team walking out to the mound to send a pitcher to the showers. Everybody knew, before Bryant said a word, that the news was bad. "Boys," he said, "I'm afraid Boston's out. Both those guys were electrocuted an hour ago. Now let's forget it and go to Canoga and show those fellers what kind of a ball club we have playing for us this season."

"God damn it," Cohn said. "We shoulda just stayed home." Profanity was punishable under the camp rules, but Bryant put his arm consolingly around Cohn's shoulders and said, "Boris, I know exactly how you feel."

They piled once more into the trucks and started for Canoga. Benjamin sat near the open end of the truck again, on the verge of vomiting after the thick sandwiches and the thermos-bottle milk. The knowledge that within an hour or so he would be playing a ball game, something that usually filled him with excitement, gave him no pleasure today, because he knew the rest of the team would be playing resentfully and that they would remember that he was the only one among them who had wanted to play the game. They would look for signs of smugness and triumph, and Benjamin knew that no matter how he behaved and whether anybody said anything about it or not, a good deal of their resentment would be turned against him. Hell, he thought, I haven't got a friend in this whole lousy camp. I'm going someplace else next summer.

They lost the game that afternoon. The whole team played stodgily. Years later, when Benjamin was in college, an unusually literate backfield coach had told him, "I don't care how much ahead you are or how good you are or how easy it is, I want players who play with *passion*. Without that, don't bother to suit up. You might as well go sit in the library on Saturdays and improve your mind. You're not going to do me or anybody else any real good out there on the field." Federov was nineteen at the time and considerably more blasé than when he reached fifty and he had smiled secretly at the coach's using a word like "passion" in connection with a boy's game. But later he had understood what the coach was talking about.

At any rate, nobody, including Benjamin, was playing with passion on that August afternoon in 1927. He didn't get a hit all day. In the eighth inning it began to rain, and he slipped and misjudged a long fly that went over his head and rolled into the woods and let in two runs that won the game for Canoga. It was the first error he had made on a fly ball all season. Nobody said anything to him when he came in from the outfield, except Bryant. "Tris Speaker," Bryant said bitterly. Speaker was the greatest center fielder of the period and the irony was not subtle. "I'm ashamed of you. I'm putting somebody else in for you. You're no damned good. And you're not in the lineup against Berkeley tomorrow, either. You're a jinx, Federov."

What a stupid man, Benjamin thought, I didn't realize how much he wanted to go to Boston. No wonder he's only second string for Syracuse. He's probably too dumb to remember the signals.

The boy who took Benjamin's place was a pudgy fifteen-year-old named Storch, who struck out on three straight called strikes without taking his bat off his shoulder, and bobbled a grounder in the outfield to let in two more runs for Canoga.

Benjamin was still too young and too committed to victory for whatever team he played on to get any satisfaction out of Storch's disgrace and for the rest of the day and evening he kept to himself, brooding and unhappy and wishing the season were over and that he was leaving for home that night.

The next morning he didn't even watch the basketball game. He took a canoe out on the Canoga lake by himself and paddled out far enough so that the cries of the spectators around the court could not be heard. He lay back in the spotty sunlight and listened to the water rippling against the canoe and read *The Saturday Evening Post*. There was a picture of an old cowboy on the cover, listening to a Victrola with a horn. The old cowboy was holding a record marked "Dreams of Long Ago" and was crying. Inside the magazine there was a story that Benjamin read with interest. *What was there to help her now? Emily asked herself rather strangely. What was to prevent her, for example, from going straight down over the hill to the gypsy camp yonder, and the violin that was calling, calling, into the dusk?*

Canoga won the basketball game, too, and Bryant lost his temper with everybody. On the long trip that afternoon to Camp Berkeley, the boys were sullen and there was no singing in any of the trucks.

FEDEROV SHIFTED A LITTLE CLOSER TO HOME PLATE because the sun was in his eyes now. Andy Roberts was still playing, but the other third baseman had been replaced by Joe Cerrazzi, whose father ran the liquor store in town. Cerrazzi had played for West Virginia a few years before and was the best ballplayer in town, and he made Federov pay attention to the game again. Cerrazzi moved constantly, went up on his toes before each play, with his hands hanging low and loose below his knees, ready for anything. During the inning he swooped in on a bunt, which he picked up with his bare hand, throwing it underhand in the same movement to nip the runner at first base. Then in the next inning, with a man on third, he cut across in front of the shortstop on a slow roller, charged the ball, kept the runner from moving with a quick feint and threw out the batter with a clothesline peg.

"Hey, Joe," Federov said, "what're you wasting your time for? The Mets need you."

"I'd rather sell booze," Cerrazzi said. "I'm an intellectual."

He was the first batter up in the next inning and connected squarely with the ball. It went in a screaming drive to dead center. Federov watched Michael turn and race, in what seemed like hopeless optimism, toward the fence that marked off the boundary of the field. At the last moment Michael leaped high against the fence, hitting hard against the wire and falling to his knees, but coming up with the ball. There were whistles of appreciation from the bench and from the few spectators and Cerrazzi came over and sat down next to Federov and said, *"There's* the one the Mets could use. Your kid. He sure likes to win, doesn't he?"

"It looks that way," Federov said. He remembered his own reaction to what the coach had said about passion when he himself had been nineteen and wondered at what age he could use the word to Michael.

"Is he going to go in seriously for playing ball?" Cerrazzi asked. "I could give him a hint or two."

"No," Federov said. "He prefers tennis."

"He's right. Tennis is something you can play all your life," Cerrazzi said, with the born athlete's solemn lack of shame about using clichés.

Federov didn't tell Cerrazzi that the only reason that Michael was playing baseball that afternoon was that he couldn't get into the town's country club because he was Jewish, or anyway half-Jewish, and the few private courts that the Jewish summer people could play on were reserved for adults on the weekends. Federov's wife, Peggy, who wasn't Jewish, was in a constant state of irritation about this and tried to keep Federov from inviting home friends of his who belonged to the Club, but Federov had long ago stopped worrying about what he considered the annoying but minor inconsistencies of American life. After Auschwitz, it was hard to be too deeply concerned because your son couldn't play two hours of doubles on a Saturday afternoon. And in the arguments he had with Peggy on the subject, he defended his Gentile friends for their passivity by reminding Peggy of all the places they themselves went to which didn't admit Negroes, despite their own theoretical absence of prejudice. "I am no longer young," he had once written to his wife in answering a letter of hers in which she had complained about what she called "the hypocrisy" of his friends at the Club. "I do not have enough anger left for all causes. I must ration it wisely."

Well, Joe Gerrazzi couldn't get into the Club either. And it had nothing to do with his religion. He couldn't get in because his father ran a liquor store. Federov wondered if Peggy would be more annoyed at being barred from playing tennis because she was married to a Jew or because of being married to a liquor salesman. I must ask her, Federov thought, the next time the damn thing comes up.

He had to squint now. There was no avoiding

41

the sun. September was approaching and the sun
was lower in the sky every afternoon. Low-sunned
September, spikes hung up, vacations over, old
outfielders playing their last games . . .

─────── **1927** ───────

ON THE MORNING OF SEPTEMBER 1ST, THEY WERE ALL
back once more in the shed of the Fall River Line
on Fulton Street. Children were being collected by
parents in loud reunions, counselors were gravely
accepting tips, aunts were exclaiming about how
wonderful little Irving or little Patrick looked, the
older boys were shaking hands with each other and
promising to meet each other during the autumn,
the director of the camp was beaming in the middle of the confusion because one more summer
had passed without a drowning or an epidemic or
poliomyelitis or an unpaid bill. The shed emptied
quickly in the rush for home, but Benjamin and
Louis were left standing there, because their parents had not yet come to pick them up. Finally,
they were the only boys left and the director assigned Bryant to stay with them to await Mr. and
Mrs. Federov's arrival.

Bryant looked far from happy at this last assignment and neither he nor Benjamin exchanged a
word with each other as they stood, a little apart,
in the shed which was suddenly eerily quiet and
cavernously large. Bryant had kept Benjamin off
the season's-end honor roll (Benjamin had learned
this from one of the waiters who had served coffee
and sandwiches at the counselors' meeting where
the votes were cast), and Benjamin had taken it
hard. He had always been high up in school, more
often than not first in his class, and had made every
weekly honor roll all season, and he ostentatiously
remained ten yards away from Bryant, wishing
him bad luck in every game Syracuse played that
fall, and ashamed that his enemy (he now considered Bryant as exactly that) was the witness of this
unprecedented callousness on the part of his mother and father. "Look," he said to Bryant fifteen
minutes after the departure of the last of the campers, "you don't have to wait. I know how to get
home. I've been to New York and back from Harrison a hundred times by myself."

"Stay where you are," Bryant said, snapping at
him. "We're waiting for your father or mother or
whatever member of your family finally remembers you're here, if it takes all day."

Louis stood there serenely, looking out at the
river, calmly munching on caramels, although it
was only nine-thirty in the morning. He had wisely
kept out a box for emergencies from the last canteen night at camp.

Their parents arrived a few minutes later, both

of them running. They had overslept, they said, the alarm had not gone off. Benjamin was furious with this foolish apology, especially since it was directed at Bryant and not at either Louis or himself. At least if it had been an accident or a death in the family or something *important*. His mother kissed him, his father embraced him and said he looked great. His mother said to Louis, "What time of the day is this to eat candy?" and kissed him ten times. His father took out a twenty-dollar bill and gave it to Bryant, who made a hypocritical show of trying to refuse it. "Take it, take it," Benjamin's father said, pressing the bill into Bryant's hand. "I know how college boys can use a few extra dollars."

Benjamin would have liked to knock the twenty dollars out of his father's hand, but he wouldn't be ready for gestures like that for another five years.

"I want to tell you, Mr. Federov," Bryant said, man-to-man, "you have two wonderful boys there. Wonderful."

Benjamin said a dirty word, under his breath, but shook hands with Bryant when Bryant came over and stuck out his hand with a false, charming smile. "It's been a great year, Tris, old feller." The echo of the afternoon at Canoga was, Benjamin knew, deliberate and malicious. "I hope we're all back together again next summer."

"Yeah," Benjamin said. "Yeah."

"Tris? Tris?" his father said puzzledly. "What's that for?"

"It's short for Tristan," said Mrs. Federov, the ex-piano teacher. "He was a knight of the Round

Table. He—well," she hesitated puritanically over
the rest of the sentence. "Well, he played around
with his friend King Arthur's wife. Her name was
Guenevere."

Israel Federov looked suspiciously at Bryant's retreating back. "What sort of name is that," he said,
"to call a thirteen-year-old boy?"

Benjamin knew that if he had said, "The center
fielder," his father would have understood, only he
would have thought it a compliment and have
liked Bryant the better for it. And Benjamin
didn't want to have to explain why it wasn't a compliment and the true nature of his relationship
with Bryant. He didn't want to talk about Bryant.
He just wanted to go home.

For many years after, the word "betrayal," in
Benjamin's mind, was linked with the handshake
in the shed and the alarm clock that had not gone
off in Harrison on the morning of September 1st,
1927.

1931-34

IT WAS THE LAST EASY SUMMER OF HIS BOYHOOD AND
youth. His father's partner turned out to be a thief

and the business went into bankruptcy in October and the Federovs never had any money again until after the war. With the failure of his father's business, Benjamin found himself scrambling, after school and during vacations, to get whatever jobs he could to feed himself, buy the necessary books for his courses, and help with a few dollars when he could, to keep the family going. He sold newspapers, he carried copy for the Newark *Ledger,* he spent a summer as a counselor in a camp in the Adirondacks, he worked as a delivery boy, and tutored backward children and performed whatever jobs were available for a hungry and inexperienced adolescent during the black years of the Depression.

When he was a freshman in college he was one of a group of students who were promised fifteen dollars apiece, plus tips, to serve as waiters on New Year's Eve at a country club in western Pennsylvania. The boy who made the arrangements was a casual friend of Benjamin's called Dyer, whose father was the manager of the country club. Since the golf course was closed and the tennis courts shut down for the winter, there was only a skeleton staff on duty and help for the huge party that was being held on New Year's Eve for the members and their guests had to be collected at random, with no questions asked about previous experience at waiting on table. All they needed was a pair of black pants and a white shirt. Black bow ties and white jackets were to be supplied by Dyer's father. The boys, fourteen in number, were to travel from the school to the country club in three borrowed cars, and they would get back late on New Year's Day.

Young Dyer, working on his father's behalf, made the whole thing seem very attractive, almost like a holiday. Dyer was a sophomore, with a little more money than most of his classmates, and was a campus politician with a smooth, confident way of talking and a quietly careless way of dressing that he hoped would make strangers believe he was an undergraduate at Princeton.

Benjamin was also involved in his first love affair that winter, with a girl who sat next to him in his English class. Her name was Patricia Forrester, and Benjamin blessed the orderly brain of the English teacher which had decreed that all students were to be seated alphabetically in front of him. Patricia was small and dark, with a pale, fine-boned, flowering face that for several years Benjamin believed to be unsurpassed in the long treasury of feminine beauty. From the first time he met her on a warm September afternoon, Benjamin had ignored all other girls and was coldly impervious to their attentions. For weeks after Pat told him that she loved him he wandered around the school grounds and through his classes in a foolish daze, forgetting where he had left his books, losing keys, turning up for the wrong courses at odd hours, staring unseeingly at his assigned reading, with Pat's face swimming, gently smiling and rich with love, between his eyes and the printed page.

They were both virgins when they met, and they kissed in doorways and in the autumn woods around the campus and in the back seats of the ramshackle cars that one or two of Benjamin's friends nagged away from their parents on Saturday nights. Even after they both realized they wanted to make love, it took weeks of planning to find a place they could use for the consummation. Benjamin lived in a dormitory; Pat lived with her mother and father and two younger sisters in an apartment a mile away from the school; the houses they went to for Saturday-night parties were always full of people, and parents in those days made a practice of returning home before midnight. The idea of going to a hotel and registering as man and wife, even if they could have afforded it, was distasteful to both of them. Their first love, they decided, could not be built on a snickering lie. Anyway, they were both sure there wasn't a hotel clerk in America who would believe that they were man and wife, no matter how many suitcases they carried into the lobby.

Benjamin was despairingly certain that if it depended upon his ingenuity he and Pat would never do more than kiss and pet in the back seats of cars until he was old enough and rich enough to marry. Eight years, he figured, bitterly. It was only when Pat took matters into her own hands and got herself and Benjamin invited to a party at the home of a girl friend of hers in New York on Thanksgiving Eve, lulling her parents' suspicions with the excuse that she wanted to stay over in the city to see the Macy parade, that Benjamin and she finally found themselves in a room together, with the door locked behind them. The New York friend's parents had gone to Atlantic City for the holiday, the friend was older than Pat and delighted to be in on the intrigue, the party was small and ended early, and the first embarrassed virginal fumbling changed quickly into joy.

Locked in the strange room that was theirs for eight hours of an autumn night, with the noises of the city drowsy and far away outside the closed and curtained windows, with the silken touch of Pat's body against his own, listening to her trustful breathing as she slept in his arms, Benjamin was sure that he could never love anyone else again in his whole life and that somehow, sometime, they would marry and spend their lives together.

They did not get up for the parade. Neither of them, as they returned that evening by train to New Jersey, trying consciously to give an appearance of unchanged innocence, regretted having missed it.

After that, having fallen onto one solution, they discovered others—a professor and his wife who wanted to get away from school for the weekend and were happy to leave their house and their small children in Benjamin's care while they were gone; a clerk at the drugstore in which Benjamin worked who liked Benjamin and was willing to lend him the key to his room occasionally; other parties, now imaginary, in New York, which freed Pat from her parents' supervision on Saturday night, when she would meet Benjamin at the Pennsylvania Hotel, where he now brazenly registered them as man and wife, using, as a joke, the name and address of the teacher of freshman English in whose class they sat demurely three hours a week, smiling secretly at each other as the teacher, an earnest, humorless young man, read students' themes aloud for criticism.

Pat's parents were mild and pleasant people who indulged their daughter and liked Benjamin, and if once in a while Benjamin had a twinge of conscience at the deception he was practicing on those hospitable and warmhearted people, he assuaged it by the knowledge that his love for their daughter was eternal and that in the end marriage would put everything aright.

Poor, overworked, shabbily dressed, uncertain of his future, at a desperate time in his country's history, Benjamin was as happy as older generations told him a tall, strong, good-looking young American should be. Only once that term were there any sharp words between Pat and himself. It was after one of the afternoons in the room of the drugstore clerk. By now, all traces of shyness, all fear of each other and fear of the obliterating intensity of their feeling had disappeared; they trusted each other absolutely, and it was inconceivable to either of them that they might ever possibly lie to each other or that he could ever conceal anything from her or she from him. They walked hand in hand along the bare, quiet, evening streets to the apartment building where Pat lived, and with no one there to watch or interfere, they kissed good night, the odor of love on their lips, the memory of the afternoon a cocoon enfolding and protecting them against the winter, real and symbolic, around them. Benjamin had read the phrase "weeping for joy" many times, always disbelieving it, but at that moment he could have wept for joy.

He kissed Pat lingeringly, then held her in his arms for a last few seconds, his cheek against hers. "Thank you," he whispered. "I wish I could tell you how grateful I am—"

Pat pulled away with an angry little wrenching movement. "Don't ever say anything like that to me again," she said.

"What is it?" he asked, puzzled. "What's the matter?"

"You make it sound as though I've done you a favor," Pat said, her voice sharp. "Love is *not* a favor. At least mine isn't. Remember that." And she turned and swept into the building.

He looked after her, stunned. Surprise Number Two, he thought. Surprise Number One had been the revelation that she loved him. He walked thoughtfully back toward school, thinking about what she had said as she pulled away from him. Love is *not* a favor. Of course not, he thought. What a tremendous girl. He arrived at the school smiling.

When, just before the Christmas holiday, he ac-

cepted Dyer's offer for the New Year's Eve job in
Pennsylvania, he knew he was going to have a
difficult explanation to make to Pat. They had
both been invited to a party for the holiday at the
apartment of Pat's girl friend in New York, with
the usual arrangement for staying over. It was
going to be a large party, the girls in evening dresses and the boys in dinner jackets, and Pat had already bought her dress and had arranged to bor-
row a dinner jacket for Benjamin from her older
married brother, who was approximately Benjamin's size. Pat was sentimental about holidays and
anniversaries, and Benjamin knew how eagerly she
was looking forward to New Year's Eve, with its
display of an elegance that until now had been
so conspicuously absent from their relationship.
Added to that, this one holiday was special and
dear to both of them, with its celebration of the
end of a year that had been the most momentous
of their lives and its ceremonial promise of loving
days to come.

As they started toward her home after the last
class before the Christmas vacation, he knew he
was going to have to tell her now and that the next
half-hour was going to be painful. It was snowing a
little, giving the ordinary little town a festive air,
and other students hurried past them exhilarated
with their freedom, voices excited, laughter easy.
Pat's face was flushed with cold and pleasure, and
she held Benjamin's arm tightly and made them
both run and slide on the snow like children.

"I have an idea," Pat said. "Let's take the bus

and go over to my brother's house and get the tuxedo. I want to see how you're going to look
and . . ."

"Pat," Benjamin said soberly, stopping and
holding her back. "I'm not going to need that
tuxedo."

"What do you mean?" She looked puzzled. "It's
all arranged."

"I know," Benjamin said. "But I can't take you
to that New Year's party."

"But we accepted," Pat said. "What's happened?"

Benjamin explained about the job at the country club and the fifteen dollars, plus tips.

Pat's face closed in, and Benjamin could see the
effort she was making to hide how deeply she was
hurt. "Fifteen dollars, plus tips," she said finally.
"Is it that important?"

Benjamin laughed ruefully. There were holes in
the soles of his shoes and he felt the snow coming
up through them; his hair was grotesquely long,
because he couldn't afford a haircut; his mother
walked more than a mile to do her shopping because she had exhausted all the family's credit in
every butcher and grocery shop in her neighborhood; his father had a temporary job, which would
end on Christmas Eve, selling toys in a Newark de-
partment store. Pat knew all this. "Pat," he said, "I
don't have to tell you the whole gloomy story all
over again, do I?"

"No," she said. There were tears in her eyes.
"Money!" she said fiercely. "I *hate* money!" She

said it so loudly that two or three of the students who were passing by looked at her curiously.

"You go to the party," Benjamin said. "You won't have any trouble finding somebody to take you." This was certainly true. There were dozens of boys and young men who still persisted in calling her to ask for dates, despite the fact that she had refused them all from the day she met Benjamin. "You'll have fun."

"I won't have fun," she said. "I'll hate anybody I go with, just because he isn't you. How can I have fun when all I want is to start the new year with you and you're hundreds of miles away waiting on table for a lot of rich miserable pigs?"

"Still," Benjamin said, "I think you ought to go."

"I'm not going," she said. Her face was white and bitter. "I'm going to go to bed at nine o'clock and stuff cotton in my ears so I won't hear the damn bells at midnight."

"Pat . . ."

"I don't want to talk about it any more," she said. She began to walk on again.

"Darling," Benjamin said, "we'll have our party on the night of the first. We'll just pretend that *our* 1932 begins one day later than everybody else's."

"All right," she said. She tried to smile. "One day later."

The group of fourteen boys, an indiscriminate sampling of freshmen, sophomores, juniors and seniors, made the bitterly cold trip through New Jersey and Pennsylvania on the morning of December 31st. When they arrived at the club, a pretentious red-brick pile, gabled and generously adorned with fake Tudor beams to deceive the members into believing they were British aristocrats, they were put to work, even before they could unpack their few belongings and see where they were to sleep. All through the leaden, icy afternoon and the numbing blackness of the early evening, they were rushing in and out of the building, assailed alternately by the north wind and waves of tropical heat from the steaming kitchen, as they carted in cases of bootleg whiskey, cases of soda water and ginger ale, cartons of food, rented chairs and rented crockery for the evening's festivities.

The first guests were due to arrive at nine o'clock and the boys were kept so busy hauling supplies that they barely had time to dress for the evening. Their rooms were a row of single cells, designed for the summer staff, on the third floor, under the roof. They ate their dinner hurriedly in the kitchen. It was a large kitchen, none too clean, and it was heaped with pots of caviar, loaves of pâté de foie gras, cold lobster and a large dead flock of roast turkeys for the feast that evening. None of this was served to the waiters. They each were given two thin frankfurters, a helping of sauerkraut, chunks of stale bread, and mugs of thin coffee. An old, shapeless Irishwoman, who spoke with a broad brogue, ran the kitchen, and she rushed over and grabbed a plate of butter from

Benjamin's hand when he went to a sideboard to bring it back to the table at which the waiters were wolfing down their meal.

"That's not for the likes of you, my lad," the old woman said, putting the butter plate decisively back on the sideboard. "Do you know what butter costs a pound these days?"

Young Dyer, who had not been seen all day, since he had gone directly to his father's home in town, came into the kitchen to hurry them up so that they would be at their places in the cloak-rooms and in the various bars before the first guest arrived. Dyer was completely transformed. He was to help his father as assistant maître d'hôtel and he was immaculately dressed in a dinner jacket, with a stiff wing collar and jeweled studs. The affable campus politician was nowhere to be seen as he looked impatiently at his watch and said, "Come on, boys, you came here to work."

"Dyer," Benjamin said, "tell that old bag I want some butter."

"She's running the kitchen," Dyer said. "There're fixed rules. Sorry. Put a move on."

"Dyer," Benjamin said, "You're a shit."

"This is no time for jokes, Federov," Dyer said.

The kitchen door opened and Dyer's father entered, He was a sallow fat man with the disappointed, suspicious eyes of a failed gambler. He, too, was handsomely turned out in a satin-lapelled dinner jacket. "The first car is coming up the driveway," he said. "Everybody at his place. *Now.*"

Benjamin struggled into his white waiter's coat and went out to his station at the downstairs bar, still chewing on his last mouthful of the tepid, stringy frankfurter.

By nine-thirty the bar was crowded. For some reason, it was decorated in nautical style: fake portholes, red and green brass running lights, model sailing vessels fully rigged in glass cases, a large ship's wheel in mahogany fitted with electric bulbs as a chandelier, all this at least two hundred miles from the sea. The nautical bar was patronized by the younger set—married couples in their mid-twenties, boys from Princeton and Yale and Harvard, all crew-cut and, to Benjamin's eyes, self-consciously lordly, who snapped their fingers at him when they wanted to order a drink. There were a great many pretty girls and young women who spoke with a flattened-A finishing-school drawl and who wore low-cut dresses that Benjamin was sure had cost at least five times as much as the dress Pat had bought for this same evening. Men and women alike, they talked of places like Newport and Hyannis and Palm Beach and what a wild weekend it had been at New Haven and how perfectly awful it was that Dahddy was set on getting a divorce again and did you hear about Ginny and that impossible South American and how *grim* they were going to feel tomorrow because they just absolutely had to catch the train at eleven o'clock for South Carolina and that would mean getting up in what was practically the middle of the night.

To Benjamin they all seemed to have known each other since birth and to be unshakably at home no matter where they were. It's a room full of Cohns, Benjamin thought, only not Jewish.

The prettiest girl there was a dark beauty in a black dress that displayed a good deal of bosom, and whose shoulder strap dropped disturbingly off her plump, tanned shoulder. She was surrounded by tall young men at the bar, and there was gust after gust of laughter from the group as they drank their bootleg whiskey-sours, and bourbon and ginger ales. The girl spoke quickly in a soft, provocative whisper, confident of her wit, using her eyes to point up her stories, enjoying the glances of the men around her at her exposed perfect breasts and her bare shoulders. She was standing near the service end of the bar, and while Benjamin was waiting next to her with his tray for a round of drinks for a party at one of the tables, he couldn't help but stare, fascinated and sick with admiration, at her naked shoulder.

" . . . so I said to him," the girl was saying, "if that's the way Harvard men behave, I'm going to try Tuskegee Institute next time." The men around her laughed very loudly, and she whipped her eyes from one to the other, making sure all tributes were being paid in full. She caught Benjamin staring at her shoulder. He raised his eyes hurriedly, and for a moment she looked at him directly and consideringly. Her glance was cold and level. He was just about as tall as any of the men in her group; he knew he was at least as good-looking, and his experience in football and boxing made him fairly sure that he could have beaten almost any of the men clustered around the bar without too much trouble. But he was wearing a waiter's white coat and he was carrying a tray and the girl's eyes became narrow and hostile. Still looking directly at him, knowing that everybody was watching her, she deliberately and contemptuously put the shoulder strap back into place. Then she turned her back on him.

He felt a hot blush of shame well up from his collar and flood his face. He would have liked to kill the girl on the spot. Instead, he counted the glasses the bartender put on his tray and made his way through the crowd toward the table he was serving.

The laughter from the bar made him tremble. He nearly spilled a drink, and a man at the table looked up at him and said sharply, "Watch what the hell you're doing, stupid."

As he went about his duties he knew he hated everybody there that night. Although he didn't want to *be* like them, he wanted, hopelessly, to *seem* like them, to feel that much at ease, that confident of blind, undeserved homage from the rest of the world.

From time to time he saw Dyer and his father as they patrolled the rooms. Now not only the Dyer of the campus, friendly and pleasant, had disappeared, but also the imperious and brusque Dyer of the kitchen. Now the Dyers, father and son, were permanently smiling, permanently bowing, obsequious, slavelike. They both gave the impression that nothing would give them deeper satisfaction than to be able to get down on their knees and kiss every polished patent-leather pump, the toe of every high-heeled satin slipper in the club that night.

At dinner, Benjamin had three tables of ten people apiece to serve. The clumsiness of inexperience was complicated for him by his inability to keep from observing a regal-looking beautiful blond girl in a white décolleté who sat at one of his tables. She couldn't have been any older than himself, but she seemed to move in a serene aura all her own, untouched by the noise and confusion around her as she filled her glass again and again throughout the meal with bootleg bourbon from one of the four bottles on the table. After the third glass, every sip she took sent a thrill of anxiety through him. You're too beautiful, he wanted to say, you're too good, you mustn't get drunk, please, for my sake, don't get drunk.

The lights in the room were dimmed for midnight, and 1932 arrived in western Pennsylvania amid the blaring of horns, drunken shouts, indiscriminate long kisses in the dark, the throwing of confetti and paper streamers, the infantilism of paper hats. Benjamin had a moment free to stand against a wall and think of himself. The entire party stood up and sang "Auld Lang Syne." Benjamin didn't sing. He thought of Pat lying in her bed, her ears stuffed with cotton against the midnight bells. He wished he had some cotton to stuff in his ears, too—and not only against church bells.

When the lights went up, the blond girl, now with her lipstick smeared, stood up and walked with perfect control past Benjamin and up the grandiose flight of steps that curved to the floor above. She disappeared, and Benjamin thought that she probably had gone to the ladies' room to repair her face. He hoped, anxiously, that she was not going to be sick. He couldn't bear the thought of that lovely face strained over a toilet bowl, that petaled soft mouth stretched by vomit. She had been gone two minutes when Benjamin saw the man who had sat next to her during dinner and who had kept filling her glass, get up and walk up the steps, too.

They were both gone thirty minutes. Then the man came down alone. He was slight, sandy-haired, about twenty years old. Benjamin had listened to scraps of his conversation during the meal and had overheard that he was a junior at Dartmouth. As the Dartmouth man passed Benjamin on his way down the steps, Benjamin saw that his bow tie, which had been a perfect black butterfly during dinner, had been clumsily retied.

Two minutes later, still regal and steady, every hair in place, the glorious white dress still unruffled, the blond girl slowly and deliberately came down the steps, in full view of the entire dining room. As she walked past the people who were now dancing in the middle of the room, Benjamin heard, or perhaps imagined he heard, a kind of rustle throughout the room, a sigh, a nervous hush between one beat of the music and the next. The girl came back to the table, sat down and nodded agreeably at the Dartmouth junior as he poured another drink for her.

Thirty minutes later, the girl stood up again and once more, with her head high and straight, made the dazzling voyage across the room and the deliberate, graceful ascent of the wide staircase. Agonized, pushing his way through the crowd of celebrants with his tray loaded with ice and cups and pots of coffee, Benjamin kept his eyes on the Dartmouth junior. The Dartmouth man didn't budge. Two minutes after the girl had disappeared up the staircase, a dark-haired man of about thirty, who had been sitting almost back to back to the girl at the adjoining table, got up from his place and mounted the stairs.

Neither the man nor the girl reappeared for almost an hour. A good many of the guests had gone home, but there were still enough people left for Benjamin to feel the rustle, the curious nervous hush, this time more intense, as the couple, now disdainfully and publicly arm in arm, descended the staircase and went onto the dance floor.

How? Benjamin thought. How can there be people like that? Where is her mother, her father, her priest, her lover? If only he hadn't been wearing the white coat of a servant, if only he hadn't felt the inhuman lack of a bridge between them, he himself would have taken the responsibility that none else would accept and would have gone over to her, spoken to her. There wasn't even a person in the entire room who would tell him her name or where she lived, so that, hidden by anonymity, emboldened by distance, he could have sat down, once safely back in school, and written her a letter imploring her to save herself.

But he did nothing. There was nothing to be done. The girl danced for a while with different men. Benjamin went into the kitchen. When he came out she was gone. A few couples still danced languidly to the music. Then the band played "Good Night, Ladies" and the night was over. The musicians packed their instruments, fled. Two boys carried a drunk covered with vomit out of the men's room. Neither Dyer nor his father was to be seen. Their last bow bowed, their last yassuh-boss smile smiled, they had driven off to their well-earned rest. The waiters straggled wearily into the kitchen. The old Irishwoman was there, locking food into the giant icebox and whiskey bottles into a small side room. There was tepid coffee out on a table for the waiters and chipped mugs and stale rolls, many of them already broken open, from the baskets on the tables. There still was no butter.

"Is this all there is to eat?" Benjamin asked the Irishwoman.

"That's all, my lad," she said. She smelled heavily of alcohol and she had a faint drunken smile on her lips. "Good nourishing bread."

"But there must be tons of turkey left over," Benjamin said.

"Tons," the old lady said.

"Why let it go to waste?" Benjamin asked. "We're starving."

"The help don't regale themselves with turkey in my kitchen," said the old lady. "Everything is fitting and proper in my kitchen."

"Why don't you stuff your turkey in a fitting and proper place in your kitchen, lady?" somebody said.

"I take that from where it comes," the old lady said contemptuously. "I don't pay any heed to the insults of servants. And that's what you are, lads. Servants. I don't care if you think you're college boys and gentlemen. I know the school you go to, I know young Dyer, with his fancy airs. He doesn't fool me any more than you boys do. Those young people out there tonight, *they're* ladies and gentlemen. Born and bred. And there isn't a one of you who'll ever be invited to the home of a single lady or gentleman who was here tonight. I'm telling you this for your own good, lads. Know your place. You'll save yourself a lifetime of grieving if you listen to an old woman who has been around quality all her life."

"Go to bed, old lady," Benjamin said wearily.

None of the other boys seemed to be listening to her as she rambled on. Numb from fatigue, they drank their coffee and mechanically ate their rolls or sat with their heads in their hands, too tired to move. "Go to bed," Benjamin said. "Or back to Ireland. Happy New Year and good night."

"Ah, you're a fresh one, aren't you?" the old lady said, still with that faint drunken smile on her lips. "I'll be interested to see where you're to be found thirty years from now. I'll go to bed, never you fear, this happy New Year. But first, I have a pleasant duty to perform. Mr. Dyer won't be in tomorrow and I'll be sleeping the good day long and I don't want to be disturbed by the likes of you. Mr. Dyer has commissioned me to give you your wages." She took a bundle of bills from the large pocket of her apron. She began to count them into piles. "Ten dollars apiece for each of you and . . ."

"Ten?" Benjamin said. "We were promised fifteen, plus tips."

"Oh, my good lad," the old lady said, "I know what you were promised. But that lad there"—she pointed at a boy called Cunningham, who was sitting with his head in his hands—"he had the grand misfortune to pour a bowl of soup on a lady's fine, expensive gown, and it's ruined forever, the lady says, and it cost five hundred dollars in a great shop in the city of Paris and who's to pay for the loss? Ten it is, lads, and you should be thankful it isn't less, due to the kindness of Mr. Dyer's good heart."

"Cunningham," Benjamin asked, "did you ruin a lady's dress?"

"I dropped a few gobs of soup on some old bag's tits. Yeah." Cunningham didn't even bother to look up. He was a frail boy, they had all been up almost twenty-four hours without any time to rest, and he sat at the table like a prizefighter who has just been knocked out and has not quite yet come around. "Five hundred dollars," he said. "My mother buys better dresses than that in Bamberger's Newark for twenty-five ninety-five."

"There you are, lads," the Irishwoman said, gesturing to fourteen neat piles on the table. "Come and get it and stop your complaining. Eleven-fifty apiece."

"What's the one-fifty for?" one of the other boys asked.

"That's each boy's share of the tips," the old lady said.

"Oh, Christ," somebody said. "Are you sure this poor white trash here tonight can afford it? Why, they may have to go without their caviar for two or three hours next year if they throw their money around like that."

"There'll be no blasphemy here in my kitchen, young man," the old lady said, "and certainly not from the likes of you." She sailed out of the kitchen into a small office near the back door and hung up her apron on a hook, closed the door, then locked it, fumbling with the key.

Cunningham began to sing "The Wearing of the Green" and was joined by some of the others. *"It's the most peculiar country that you have ever seen,"* the boys sang, their voices hollow and mocking in the cold, echoing kitchen, *"For they're hanging men and women, for the wearing of the green—"*

"Not enough," Cunningham said.

Angrily the old lady turned around. She staggered a little as she came up to Cunningham and shook her finger at him. "I'll have no slurs on the Irish either, lad, I warn you."

"He's Irish, lady," somebody said.

"I know what kind of Irish," said the old lady. "Scum." She lurched out, and they heard her walking unevenly down the hall to her bedroom.

"Well," Benjamin said, standing up, "I never had more fun in my life. I'm going to bed."

They decided they'd all leave by eleven in the morning and climbed the three flights heavily to the servants' rooms under the roof.

When Benjamin got to his door, it was locked. Sleepily, he tried to figure out how that could have happened. He knew he had left the key in the door when he went down before dinner, because there was nothing in the room that anybody could possibly have wanted to steal. But there was no doubt about it now. It definitely was locked. He tried to throw his weight against the door, but it held. He went into the next room where Cunningham, too tired to undress, lay sprawled, with the light on, across his cot.

Benjamin told Cunningham about the door and opened the window of the room to see if there was some way he could get to his own window three feet away. A polar wind howled in through the open window and Cunningham moaned. There was a rain gutter that looked secure along the edge of the sloping roof and the roof itself had wooden shingles on it that would give good purchase for fingers and Benjamin stepped out gingerly, testing the gutter. "Well," he said to Cunningham, "tell the boys I died game."

Cunningham heaved himself up from the cot with what seemed to be the last ounce of energy left in his body and leaned out the window to watch as Benjamin inched his way along, trying not to look down at the ground forty feet below him. "Hurry up, for Christ's sake," Cunningham said. "I'm freezing."

Benjamin reached his window and tried to open it. It was locked. The wind whistled through his thin shirt (they had left their white jackets and bow ties in the kitchen). The shade was down, although he was sure he hadn't drawn it in the few minutes he had spent in his room before the night's work began. "The hell with it," he said to Cunningham. He took out his handkerchief, wrapped it around his fist, and broke the top pane of glass, then reached in, turned the lock mechanism, lifted the bottom half of the window, ran up the shade, and crawled in. Safely inside, he leaned out and said to Cunningham, "Ok, go to sleep."

Cunningham closed his window. Benjamin went to the door and flicked on the light. Then he turned and surveyed the room, which was shaking now with the wind that roared in through the broken pane. The bed had been used. The one blanket was in a heap on the floor, the sheet was crumpled, half on the bed, half on the floor. There were lipstick stains all over the sheet and pillowcase.

The blond girl, Benjamin thought. The drunken blond whore. Maybe she was hunting a third lay and that's why she locked the door and took the key. For future use. His comb and brush were on the floor. He picked them up. There were two or three fine pale hairs in his comb. No wonder she looked so neat when she came down the stairs. For a moment, he considered wrapping himself in his overcoat and sleeping on the floor. No, he thought, fighting an insane and impotent rage. I won't give the bitch the satisfaction. He hung his coat as best as he could over the broken window. It kept out some of the wind, but not much. It must have been at least ten below zero outside. Shivering, he picked up the sheet and made the bed. The lipstick stains were in some strange places, he noted, and there was the stain of semen and its distinctive odor, faint but probing. He put out the light and lay down in his clothes, after taking his shoes off. He pulled the thin blanket over him. As his body warmed the sheets the odor of the bed, the musty odor of the straw mattress, the fragrance of perfume, the womb and vagina and semen smell of sex, rose to his nostrils. Exhausted as he was he couldn't sleep. As he lay there, trying to breathe through his mouth so as not to smell the disturbing mixture of odors, trying not to recreate in his mind what must have happened in this bed while he was downstairs, he realized that, with all his loathing, he wanted the girl who had used his bed in which to make love with two men that night and that if she came through the door he would take her in his arms if she would have him.

From that moment he knew he was going to search for girls like that, for girls like the one in the black dress who had pulled up her shoulder strap when she noticed that he was watching her, that he wanted a hundred girls he had seen downstairs during the course of the night, and that in the long run he was going to sleep with as many of them as he could. At the same moment he knew he was never going to marry Pat and that, for a longer or shorter period of his life, he was going to be promiscuous and probably perverse and, for a long time and perhaps forever, incapable of fidelity.

"Ah, God," he said aloud. He got up and put on the light. He sat on the edge of the bed, shivering, but wide awake. Suddenly, he realized that he was famished. He had to have something to eat or faint from hunger. Then he remembered the old lady's key. She had left it in the door of her office next to the kitchen when she had turned angrily on Cunningham as he started to sing "The Wearing of the Green."

Benjamin put on his shoes, tried the door. It still held. He looked around the room for something to break the door down with. There was an old putter with a broken handle lying in the corner of the room, left there by some caddy or athletic waiter the summer before. Benjamin picked up the putter and began hacking at the top panel of the door, unmindful of the noise. He banged crazily at the thin wood and soon it began to splinter and holes began to open up. With his bare hands, Benjamin ripped out sections of the panel. A jagged, sharp piece of wood ripped his hand and there was blood on the door and on his clothes, but he didn't stop.

Nobody seemed to have heard the noise. All the boys were so exhausted you could have shot cannons off in their ears without waking them. Besides, the howl of the wind around the eaves and through cracks in the walls kept the whole floor in a turmoil of creaks and haunted whistles. Soon there was a hole in the door big enough to crawl through. Benjamin lowered his small bag through the hole, put on his jacket and overcoat and climbed out.

He went down through the darkened building. On the floor below, where there were several guest rooms that were locked for the winter, there was no sound. As he descended the stairway, the smell of spilled whiskey, dancers' sweat, stale food assailed him from the dining room. He found the kitchen and turned on the light. He left blood on the switch.

The key was in the door to the small office. He turned it, went in. He saw the old lady's apron hanging on the hook. He reached into the apron pocket. The ring of keys was there. He took them, leaving a stain of blood on the cloth, and tried the icebox padlock. On the third try, the key worked. The icebox was enormous and crammed with food. He left the door open, then went to the little room where the liquor was locked away. He found the key for that, too, and opened the door. There were at least ten cases of whiskey there and dozens of half-full bottles. A wild smile contorted his face as he looked at the treasure. He took an opened bottle of whiskey and put it on the big table. Then he went to the icebox and took out a platter of turkey, a large can of caviar, a slab of butter, a pound loaf of pâté de foie gras. He arranged them with crazy precision in a row next to the whiskey bottle, then went to the bread bin, which was unlocked, and took out six rolls. He found a fork and a knife and a mug and sat down, making himself move slowly for maximum enjoyment of the meal, and began to eat. He ate four large helpings of caviar on rolls, spread with a mixture of blood and butter. He ate half the loaf of pâté, washing down each mouthful with raw whiskey. It was the first time he had ever eaten pâté de foie gras and he didn't know what the delicious black slivers embedded in it were called. The next day Cunningham told him they were called truffles. He made three sandwiches piled with slices of breast of turkey and ate them. He made another sandwich and munched on it as he climbed up to the top floor again and woke up all the boys one by one, shaking them and making sure they were awake enough to understand him when he told them what he proposed to do. In all the mean, bare rooms of the top floor the boys got out of bed, dressed, took their bags with them and stole down to the kitchen.

"No food to be taken along," Benjamin warned them. "Only liquor. It's all bootleg and they can't go to the police about it."

So the boys ate pâté, caviar, turkey, ice cream,

lobster, potato salad, in any order that was conven-
ient as they reached into the icebox and rifled the
whiskey cases and filled their bags and gunny sacks
and cardboard cartons with the bottles.

"Tonight," Benjamin said, thinking of Pat,
"we're going to have ourselves a *real* New Year's
Eve party."

It was six-thirty in the morning when they tip-
toed out of the building to where the three cars
were parked under a shed behind the kitchen. It
was pitch-dark, but they didn't put on any lights as
they loaded the cars. In five minutes they were
ready to go. The engines coughed in the pre-dawn
cold, caught, and they rolled down the driveway,
catching the huge Pennsylvania-Tudor pile of the
club building momentarily in the glare of the
headlights as they took a curve. England, my England, Benjamin thought sardonically, as the car
lights picked out the dark beams. Then the
building disappeared in the darkness and they
sped toward home.

Most of the boys, when they weren't spelling the
drivers, slept. But Benjamin couldn't sleep. He
had never stolen anything in his life. Now I am a
thief, he thought. He knew that later he would
have to come to terms with this idea, as he would
with the idea of the girl who had used his bed and
the girl who had made him blush. But for the moment he was too tired, too inflamed by a hatred he
had never known he could feel for anyone, to
make any judgment on himself.

They held the party that night, but it was an anti-climax. They were all too exhausted to enjoy it, although there was a moment of laughter when they drew straws to see who would beat up Dyer when he came back to school after the holidays and a boy called Swinton, who was the best student in school, but was blind without his glasses and twenty-five pounds lighter than Dyer, came up with the short straw. So the problem of what to do with Dyer was postponed for more sober discussion.

Pat looked beautiful and happy, and Benjamin tried to match her mood. "Isn't it nice," she said, "to have our own private New Year." Benjamin danced with her and went into the kitchen with her to kiss her a true and sensual Happy New Year. But he knew he had already betrayed her, even if the actual act of betrayal was years in the future.

The night had put its mark on Benjamin and he knew it. He was ashamed of himself. Filthy people had behaved filthily to him and he had become filthy himself.

Nobody ever hit Dyer and he didn't say anything about what had happened at the country club, and in his junior year he was elected president of his class.

Eighteen months after the New Year's party, Pat's family moved to Oregon and she had to go along with them. She and Benjamin wrote to each other for a while, but it was no good, and by that time Benjamin had taken up with any number of other girls, none of them as good of heart or as brave and honest as Pat, but with whom he could go to bed without love or the pretense of love. In his imagination at that period, he thought of himself as mounting a curving ornate staircase over and over and over again.

After he got out of school and had moved to New York, Benjamin had an affair with a girl named Prentiss, who, it turned out, had been at the New Year's Eve party in Pennsylvania. Neither of them remembered having seen each other that night and, from Benjamin's description, the girl could not identify either the blond who had used his bed or the pretty dark bitch at the bar.

Miss Prentiss, it turned out, had her own peculiarities. She was the daughter of a Methodist minister from a small town near Scranton, with a face and manner of speaking that Benjamin's mother would have called "refined." But after the affair, which had lasted nearly three months and had been conducted in a fashion that Mrs. Federov would have never called refined, Miss Prentiss, naked and sipping straight bourbon on the edge of her wide double bed, asked Benjamin to marry her. He was making twenty-three dollars a week and going to night school to study drafting and, while he enjoyed seeing Miss Prentiss from time to time and sharing her bed and her bourbon, he could not see himself marrying her. She was pretty in a faded blond way, but given to neurotic bouts of anger and tears and insisted that he eat no meat when he went out with her, because she was a vegetarian and could not stand the sight even of a slice of chicken on a platter. She was the first girl he'd ever known who went to a psychiatrist and, in exchange for the lovemaking and the whiskey, he had to listen to endless reports from the couch, mostly about her father and his sermons and dreams of animals dying in their own blood.

"Marriage?" Benjamin asked. "Are you out of your mind? Do you know how much money I make a week?"

"I don't care," Miss Prentiss said, turning her refined pale eyes and refined watery breasts in his direction as he lay, with the sheet up to his waist, in the rumpled bed. "I have a little money. And when Daddy dies I'll have quite a bit more."

"Have I ever told you I love you?" Benjamin asked, seeking safety in brutality.

"Do you love me?"

"No."

"No," Miss Prentiss said. She sipped calmly at her bourbon. "But I need you."

"Not that much, you don't," Benjamin said, wondering how he could get up and dressed and out of the apartment without seeming like a cad.

"You don't know," she said. "I have great difficulty in being satisfied. Sexually, I mean."

"I hadn't noticed," he said.

"Not with you," she said. "That's the point. With other men. The torment I've gone through."

"What's so special about me?" Benjamin asked, half-suspicious and half-flattered and not averse to having his dearest illusions about himself confirmed.

"You're a Jew," she said. "I can only have an orgasm with a bestial Jew."

"Let's talk it over some other time, darling," Benjamin said, getting out of his side of the bed and starting hurriedly to get dressed. "It's late and I still have two hours work to do before I go to sleep."

As he walked toward the subway down the tree-lined street in Greenwich Village where Miss Prentiss lived, a street probably teeming with bestial Jews, Benjamin shook his head. That country club in Pennsylvania, he thought. What a collection!

He was living in New York because of another woman—a woman he had seen only once for fifteen minutes. It was in a public hospital in Trenton. He had just been graduated from college and had managed to pass the examinations for teaching in grade school in the New Jersey state system and had been called with a hundred other candidates for a physical examination. The doctor turned out to be a short dumpy woman with thick-lensed glasses who looked at the half-naked young men she had to pass on as though they were all suffering from a loathsome disease. Another doctor had already checked Benjamin's heart, lungs, and eyesight and had noted that Benjamin had had measles and whooping cough and did not limp or have any crippling deformities. The lady doctor merely was weighing and measuring the candidates. When it was Benjamin's turn, she looked a long time at the scale as it came to rest. Her expression was one of distaste and her voice was disapproving as she called out, "One eighty-seven," to the clerk at the table next to the scale.

Benjamin stepped off the scales and picked up his shirt, trousers and shoes, wondering what school he would be assigned to and how long it would be before he could give up teaching for something for which he was better fitted.

"I'm afraid you'll be rejected, Mr. Federov," the lady doctor said.

"What?" Benjamin asked incredulously. The last time he had been sick had been at the age of six.

"You're obese, Mr. Federov," the lady doctor said.

"Obese," he repeated stupidly. He looked down at his powerful hard arms, his tucked-in, narrow waist, at the long, granite-hard halfback's legs. He was twenty-one years old and he could tear telephone books in half with his bare hands and run the mile in well under five minutes, and in the last baseball game of the year he had hit a home run over a fence 350 feet away. "Obese," he said. "There isn't an ounce of fat on me." He was ready to cry with wounded vanity. The summer before, when he had been working as a counselor, the girl counselors had taken a vote on the man with the best body in camp and he had been designated. And now this dumpy little woman with glaucous

eyes and bad breath and breasts like market bags
was telling him he was obese.

"According to the chart," the lady doctor said,
enjoying his humiliation as she would enjoy the
humiliation of any man who fell, even momentarily, under her power, "according to the chart, a
man of your age and height should not weigh more
than one hundred and sixty-five pounds."

"But I'm a football player," Benjamin said,
feeling foolish. "That's the way football players're
built."

"You're not in college any more," the lady doctor
said crisply. "You're not going to be pampered
here just because you can throw a football every
Saturday."

"But I need the job, ma'am," Benjamin said.
The depression was on and there were twenty ap-
plicants for every job in the country, and a job
made the difference between eating and not eating. "I passed the examinations and I've been
counting on—"

"You didn't pass *this* examination, Mr. Federov," the woman said. "I'm afraid you'd better
move on. There are a lot of people waiting."

Benjamin looked around him wildly, searching
for an argument, any argument, to impress this
miserable woman, keep her judgment on him from
being final, concluded, catastrophic. The boy in
front of him, a classmate of Benjamin's named
Levy, was standing on the other side of the scale,
safely through, snickering. Levy was a short, nar-

row-shouldered boy with sickly oysterish skin marked by the livid scars of years of carbuncles. His chest was concave, he was knock-kneed, his legs and arms were like sticks, his eyes were protruding and yellowish. With all that, you'd have thought he would have to be brilliant in his work, but he wasn't. He was one of the stupidest boys in the class and had just barely passed the written examination. Benjamin had never liked him, and he liked him considerably less at this moment, as Levy stood next to the scale, smirking, sweating unpleasantly in his oyster-colored skin.

"Him!" Benjamin said, pointing ungallantly at Levy. "You pass *him*, that—that scarecrow—and you flunk me. What sort of deal are you running here, anyway?"

"Hey," Levy said, whining, "leave me out of this."

"Mr. Levy is perfectly normal," the woman said crisply. "Next."

"*He's* normal?"

"Officially normal," the woman said.

"And what am I?" Benjamin asked. "Officially a freak?"

"Nobody said that, Mr. Federov," the woman gestured toward the next boy in line. "You are officially obese."

"But there must be *something* I can do," Benjamin said, standing there feeling ridiculous, fighting for his livelihood, dressed only in underpants and socks and holding his clothing in his hand, with fifteen other half-naked men in the room grinning at the scene.

"You can lose twenty-two pounds, Mr. Federov," the lady doctor said, "and come back here in three months."

"I'd have to cut off a *leg* to lose twenty-two pounds," Benjamin shouted, losing his temper.

"That's up to you, Mr. Federov," the lady doctor said. "Next."

He went dazedly out of the hospital, wanting to scream obscenities in the corridors or join the Communist Party or found an organization with the purpose of keeping women out of the medical profession. He sat down in the June sunlight on a park bench and put his head in his hands to contemplate the ruin of his life. As usual, his family was living with all the doors locked, the telephone turned off and the blinds down, so that bill collectors would gain no entrance. His parents had been proud that he had passed his examination and was now entering that Jewish realm of aristocrats, the world of scholars, even though his actual job would entail teaching eight-year-old children how to spell and solve arithmetical problems involving half a dozen pears and the price of ten oranges. But a teacher's pay in those days was respectable, and they had all looked forward to being able to live with the shades up and the telephone connected.

Benjamin groaned on his bench. He was not

going back to that entrenched house that night
without a job, no matter what the job was. He had
a copy of *The New York Times* in his pocket and
he took it out and spread out the Help Wanted
pages. He made some marks with a pencil, then
went to the station and bought a ticket to New
York.

It was nearly eight o'clock, but still daylight,
when he turned down the shabby street of connected one-family stucco houses on which he lived.
Like his own, and for the same reasons, almost half
the houses looked permanently shut and aban-
doned. He walked carefully on the other side of
the street from his own house, peering cautiously
for secreted bill collectors and summons-servers,
then hurried across the street and let himself in
with his key.

His father was sitting in the living room in his
shirt sleeves and with his shoes off. Israel was peddling household gadgets from door to door, and it
meant walking miles and miles each day on blazing
pavements, and the first thing he did when he got
home at night was take his shoes off. Israel had an
evening newspaper on his lap, but the electricity
had been off for a month and it was too dark to
read with the shades down, and he was just sitting
there in a threadbare upholstered chair, staring
reflectively at a photograph on the opposite wall of
Louis and Benjamin that had been taken on the
beach when Benjamin was six years old. As Benjamin came into the room, he was sure that his fa-

ther was thinking the same thing as himself—that it would be wonderful if Benjamin was again six years old and everything remained to be done all over again—differently.

By now, Benjamin could tell from the way his father sat in the chair what kind of a day Israel had had. When he had sold more than five dollars worth of the household gadgets during the day, Israel sat hopefully, his head up. His head was not up tonight.

The living room gleamed from Sophie Federov's ministrations. Unable to halt the Depression, powerless to change the economy of the country or redeem the family fortunes in Wall Street, Sophie Federov fought the malevolence of the times in her own manner, in her own home. She scrubbed, she polished, she swept and washed and kept everything in place to the last precise half-inch in furious defiance of the chaos that threatened each day to engulf them all.

The room looked like a room in a museum. Exhibit B a lower-middle-class living room, furniture by Grand Rapids, with various silver objects out in pawnshops, *circa* 1934.

Benjamin heard the sounds of his mother preparing dinner in the kitchen. He had hoped that by some miracle she would not be home this evening. But she was home. She was always home.

"Hi, Pop," Benjamin said.

His father's head went up. He smiled. When Israel looked at his sons, for a moment or two, anyway, it was a good day.

Mrs. Federov came into the room, an apron, starched and immaculate, tied around her trim waist. Benjamin kissed her and held her a fraction of a second longer than usual in his arms.

"What's for dinner?" he asked, postponing.

"Something special. Hamburger," his mother said ironically. "Well, when do you go to work?"

"Tomorrow," Benjamin said.

"Tomorrow?" His mother was surprised. "I thought the summer session didn't begin until July."

"Sit down, Mom," Benjamin said.

"I don't have to sit down," she said. She was bracing herself for tragedy already. "What happened?"

"I have a job," Benjamin said. "But not in the school system."

"What do you mean, not in the school system? You passed the examination, didn't you?"

"I thought so," Benjamin said.

"You thought so?" his mother said sharply. "Don't talk in riddles."

"I didn't pass the physical examination today in Trenton," Benjamin said.

A look of alarm crossed his mother's face. She gripped his arm tightly and stared into his eyes. "Tell the truth," she said. "They found something in the hospital. What is it? Tuberculosis? You have a bad heart? What?"

"Nothing like that," Benjamin said. "I . . . I'm overweight. The technical term is 'obese.' "

"Overweight. Obese?" His mother sounded bewildered. "What are they, crazy in Trenton? Did you hear that, Israel? In Trenton they say your son is obese."

"The government," Israel said resignedly. "What can you expect?"

Mrs. Federov stepped back and eyed Benjamin sharply. "You're not joking, are you? One of your bad jokes, Ben?"

"I'm not joking. That's what they said."

"But you have the body of a god," Mrs. Federov said. "They should be built like you, those maniacs in Trenton."

This was not the day Benjamin wanted to hear that he was built like a god, not even from his mother. But he couldn't repress a smile at the thought of the lady doctor waking up in the morning to find herself built like him.

"They have a chart," he explained wearily. "On the chart I'm twenty-two pounds overweight."

"But you're a football player, that's the way football players get, didn't you explain that?"

"I explained it," Benjamin said. "It makes no difference. They go by the chart."

"Football," Mrs. Federov said bitterly. "You had to play football. You wouldn't listen to your mother. Now see." She turned on Israel, sunk into his chair. "And you, you encouraged him. All these years. Now are you satisfied?"

Israel hunched his shoulders a little. It was a habit that had grown on him since he lost his business.

"We sit in the dark because we can't pay the

electricity, and your son is twenty-two pounds overweight," Mrs. Federov said to her husband, "and all you can do is sit in your chair with your shoes off."

At that moment, Benjamin decided he was not going to marry unless he had one million dollars in the bank. Or maybe two million dollars.

His mother whipped around toward him, a small, straight, beautiful, fierce, indomitable woman, keeping a family together through one catastrophe after another, keeping things going with an iron ferocity of will, an unconquerable, spotless firmness of spirit in the dark, polished house that was her castle, her battlefield, her world. "Now," she said to her son, "what was that about going to work tomorrow?"

"I went to New York this afternoon," Benjamin said, "and I got a job."

"What kind of job?" his mother asked suspiciously.

"It pays eighteen dollars a week," Benjamin said.

"What kind of job?" his mother said.

Benjamin took a deep breath. "Shipping clerk," he said. "In an electric-appliance firm on West Twenty-third Street."

"Oh, my God. A shipping clerk. My son." Mrs. Federov began to cry.

"What's there to cry about?" Benjamin said crossly, because now he would have liked to be able to cry, too.

"High school, college, A's and B's all the way through, starving to buy books, and you say what's wrong with being a shipping clerk."

"It's not forever," Benjamin said. "I'll go to night school. I'll study drafting and engineering—"

"I know what you'll do," his mother said through her tears. "You'll associate with hoodlums, you'll get drunk on Saturday nights, you'll go to whorehouses with all the others, you'll wheel carts through the streets to the post office like a day laborer, you'll forget you ever read a book, you'll marry a cheap little factory girl and live like pigs, and your children will grow up to be shipping clerks just like you. I won't let you do it."

"Oh, Christ," Benjamin said, furious in his turn now, "when are you going to get over the idea that everybody who works with his hands is a hoodlum?"

"I won't get over the idea," Mrs. Federov sobbed. "Because it's true, it's true. Israel," she cried, "aren't you going to say something about it?"

His father was silent for a moment. Then he shrugged. "Sophie," he said, "he's a grown man. The times're difficult. I have faith in him."

"You will not leave this house tomorrow to work as a laborer," Mrs. Federov said to Benjamin. "That is not what I gave my life for."

"Mom . . ." Benjamin said wearily. "Be realistic. We're sitting here in the dark because the lights're turned off. There're six million unemployed. They're not waiting for your son. I want to be able to go over to the wall and push a button and have the lights come on in this house. And I'll do anything—*anything* for it."

"There's no sense," his mother wept, sitting straight on the edge of a wooden chair, her hands clutched in her lap. "There's no sense in the whole thing."

He didn't have the courage to tell her the worst thing—that if she tried to reach him on the telephone at his place of work, she would be told that nobody by the name of Federov was employed by that firm. He had given his name as Bradley Faye, because in the advertisement in *The New York Times* it had said that only white Gentiles need apply.

---------------- 1964 ----------------

"HI"

Federov blinked. The dark, polished, threadbare room drifted away. Leah Stafford was standing in front of him along the third-base line. She gestured toward the empty bench alongside him. "Is that seat taken?"

"Sit down." Federov tapped the board with his

right hand. Leah climbed the two lower planks and sat down. They didn't kiss or shake hands. Leah was well over forty, but didn't look it. She had deep copper-colored hair that she wore long, and a creamy complexion, now being preserved from the sun by a wide blue straw hat that added shifting sea-colors to her large green eyes. She was tall, slender, with long legs, and was one of those women who seemed to have been created especially for the styles of the middle of the twentieth century. Now she was wearing cream-colored, closefitting slacks and a loose, lightweight green sweater and blue sandals to match the hat. Summertime, Federov thought, admiring the color scheme. They had been lovers for several years, during and after the war, between her divorce from Bill Ross and her marriage to John Stafford.

"I didn't know you were a baseball fan," Federov said.

"I'm not," Leah said. "The younger generation." She made a gesture with her head toward the field. Young Johnny Stafford was playing right field. He was among the worst players in town and always was put in right field, with all his teammates hoping there wouldn't be any lefthanders in the opposing lineup who would hit in that direction. "I promised Johnny I'd pick him up and take him home."

"Where's John?" Federov asked.

"Home," Leah said, "preparing the plans for the next civil war."

Federov laughed. John Stafford, whose ancestors

had helped found the town in the eighteenth century, had been born to wealth, educated at the most imposing schools, served on the board of a bank his family had controlled for more than a hundred years and, with all this, worked tirelessly on missions for the government, on committees and foundations and school boards for such things as aid to refugees, the implementation of civil-rights programs, the assignment of scholarships to bright boys from poor homes, and all sorts of thankless but necessary civic tasks. Stafford dressed in the best traditions of his class, drank like a gentleman, and was, as Leah had once put it, insanely generous and hospitable. When he married Leah, he had quietly resigned from the Golf and Tennis Club, because she was Jewish, although nobody in the club would ever have challenged him on the subject and Leah herself had protested at length against her husband's meticulous devotion to his conscience. Federov considered Stafford one of his best friends, and they saw each other at least two or three times a week, both in the city and down here at the shore. Federov had named him as guardian for Michael and his daughter in case he and Peggy were killed in an accident or died before Michael attained his majority. In the normal course of events, Federov would have asked Louis to assume the responsibility for the children, but with all the love between the brothers and all of Federov's appreciation for Louis's qualities, he couldn't face up to the thought of his son and daughter being in on some of scenes with various wives, ex-wives, mistresses, and future wives that occurred with disheartening regularity in the tumult of Louis's dealings with women.

"Are you coming over tonight?" Leah asked.

"Are we invited?"

"Yes."

"I'll have to ask Peggy," Federov said. "She's my social secretary. Will it be amusing?"

"No," Leah said, squinting out toward where her son was wheeling drunkenly under a high fly ball. "My advice is, don't come. My, that boy plays badly," she said as her son dropped the ball, then picked it up and threw to the wrong base. "The poor dear."

"Why won't it be amusing?" Federov asked.

"John's cooked up a new, brilliant idea he's going to pop tonight. He wants to set up a loan association of local homeowners who'll help deserving Negroes buy houses here."

"That doesn't sound like such a poor idea," Federov said.

"You're just as bad as he is," Leah said. "I'm going to start a committee with Peggy—The South Shore Association of Christian and Jewish Ladies for the Advancement of Medieval Behavior." Leah had been born Leah Levinson, but if you were as beautiful as that it took more imagination than Leah possessed to believe that people could be damaged in any way just because they had a name like Levinson.

"You're awful," Federov said.

"Isn't it the truth?" She turned and looked with

just the slightest intention of flirtation at Federov. They had stopped being lovers long ago, but even now she amused herself by proving all over again that he was not immune to her.

"Cut it out, lady," Federov said.

"Cut what out?" she asked innocently.

"You know."

"You still being a bad boy?" she asked.

"No," Federov said. "And if I were, I wouldn't tell you."

"Old age?"

"Maturity," Federov said.

They watched their two sons, almost the same age, playing side by side in the outfield. Federov could tell, even at that distance, that Michael disdained Johnny Stafford. Any ball Michael could possibly reach, even though Johnny would hardly have to move a step to catch it, Michael raced over to field. When Johnny called over to say something to Michael, Michael didn't even turn his head to answer. And when Johnny dropped the fly ball, Michael looked up to heaven in a style that Federov recognized from disputes at home and that meant, in thirteen-year-old sign language, "Oh, my dear God, why am I being thus afflicted?"

Federov shook his head regretfully. Michael's attitude hadn't changed anything in his own relationship with John Stafford, but it was a constant, irremediable small annoyance. Federov found Johnny a charming boy, well-mannnered like his father, with the imprint of his mother's beauty evident, but clearly masculinized. But by his desperate activities in right field, Johnny forfeited, at least for the years of his adolescence and possibly for his whole life, any claim on Michael's friendship or even tolerance. I'm going to speak to the little bastard at least once more about it, Federov thought, knowing in advance that it was hopeless.

"It's funny, isn't it?" Leah asked. She had a voice that went with her particular kind of beauty —low, promising, musical, with a hidden echo of malice.

"What's funny?"

"Us sitting here," Leah said, "and the two kids out there. By different fathers, according to rumor."

"Leah," Federov said with all the firmness he could command, "don't be impossible."

Leah chuckled. "It's one of the pleasures of my life," she said, "getting a rise out of you. I can do it every time, can't I?"

"No," Federov said, lying.

"Liar," Leah said.

They had met in 1935, just after Leah had married a friend of Federov's called Ross. Leah was sixteen when she married. Nobody was surprised that she had married at the age of sixteen. As her mother had said at the wedding, "I thank God we managed to wait this long. I was afraid she was going to get married before she was twelve."

Federov had seen the couple off and on for about a year, then the Rosses had moved to Detroit and he hadn't seen Leah again until 1945 in Paris, where Leah, now divorced, was serving as a Red Cross girl, interfering with the conduct of the war. Federov was on leave for a week, and it was when he went into the Red Cross Enlisted Men's Club on the Boulevard des Capucines that he found that the coffee and doughnuts he had come in for were being served to him by Leah Ross.

He was married to Peggy by this time, but the first thing he thought when he saw Leah was, I was wrong not to be in the same city the day her final decree of divorce was handed down.

───────── 1942 ─────────

PEGGY'S FATHER WAS A COLONEL IN THE MEDICAL Corps in Georgia, where Benjamin was being trained as an infantryman.

Peggy was twenty that year, blond, not very tall, her eyes so deeply blue that in some lights they appeared violet. She wore her thick, rough hair cut short, almost like a boy's; her body was lithe, with a hint of later fullness. Her legs were rounded, but athletically firm, and Benjamin, who had been spoiled a little by the ease with which he had drifted into one affair after another with some of the prettiest women in New York, was surprised to find that he thought, in all sobriety, that Peggy's legs, with their healthy sensuality, were the most charming legs he had ever seen on a girl. At twenty, Peggy was startlingly pretty; by the age of thirty she would be beautiful.

Benjamin met her on a tennis court in the garden of some friends of his parents, a middle-aged couple by the name of Bronstein, who had moved south from New York and who ran a prosperous men's clothing store in town and who invited him to their house every time he was released for a few hours from camp.

Peggy's parents had rented the house next to the Bronstein's. The first time Benjamin saw Peggy was when she came through a gate in the hedge that divided the two properties. She was wearing a short tennis dress, and her legs were tanned, and as she came toward the court where Benjamin was rallying desultorily with the Bronstein's fifteen-year-old son, Benjamin purposely hit the ball into the net so that he could watch Peggy approach. He stared at her unashamedly, swept by a nameless nostalgia at the image of the young girl in the short white dress coming through the green, summery hedge, a negation of death, wars, all the angular, tortured, masculine world of armies.

She played very good tennis, too, hitting all-out in the California style (her family were San Franciscans) and moving swiftly around the court, with her brief skirt flaring as she ran up to the net to reach for shots. When she missed a smash, she would shake her head and say in mock despair, "Peggy Woodham, you play like a *girl!*" She was not easy to beat. The first set she and Benjamin played against each other on that hot Sunday morning in Georgia, Benjamin only managed to win by 6–4. She shook his hand gravely at the net and said, "I never thought I'd be beaten by somebody from *New York*. And especially with a backhand like yours."

"What's the matter with my backhand?" Benjamin asked.

"It's a mockery," she said, teasing him. "Pure mockery. It's a PFC of a backhand."

"You're rank-happy," Benjamin said. Somehow, from the first moment, they spoke to each other as though they had known each other for years. "Just because your father is a colonel," Benjamin said. He had learned quite a bit about her during the course of the morning. Her father was the commanding officer of the surgical section at the camp hospital; she worked in a bookshop in town; she had just got her BA from Stanford; she had been engaged to be married to a star football player and had broken it off because her fiancé had turned out to be a nasty man; she had an inferiority complex because her mother was one of the most beautiful women in San Francisco. She spoke gaily, swiftly, with a Western openness and directness and, by the time the morning was over and they went into the Bronstein house for lunch, Benjamin was thinking. It's a lucky thing there's a war on; otherwise I'd be planning to marry her. He was twenty-eight years old by then and he had carefully avoided getting married. For one thing, since the episode with Pat in college, no woman had appealed to him as a possible wife. For another, he was determined not to enter marriage as a poor man. Marriage was tough enough without that.

After lunch Peggy's father came over and they played doubles with the Bronstein's son. Patrick Woodham was a wiry bald man with a face and manner made for command. When Patrick Woodham was ten years old you would have known that if there ever was a war there would be eagles on his shoulders. Some colonels are made, some are born. Patrick Woodham was born a colonel. He also played a formidable game of tennis, and he and the Bronstein boy beat Benjamin and Peggy three sets in a row before they quit, because Colonel Woodham had to get back to the hospital.

Benjamin couldn't tell whether the Colonel liked him or not. Woodham had a brusque, authoritative manner with everybody except his daughter. She was an only child, and he spoke to her with an indulgent tenderness that made Benjamin like the man, even if the man didn't like him.

As they sat on the bench in the shadow of an oak by the side of the court, recovering from the last set, Woodham said to Peggy, "Put on your sweater. You'll catch cold like that."

"I'm boiling," Peggy said.

"Put on your sweater," Woodham said.

"Yes, Colonel," Peggy said. "Yes, sir, Colonel."

Some day, Benjamin thought, looking at the fined-down hard man smiling with love and amusement at the girl, some day I must have a daughter.

They made love three weeks later, on a Saturday night, in the warm dark garden behind the tennis court. Peggy was not a virgin. "Remember," she said later, enjoying her own candor, "I have a BA from Stanford. They don't give degrees to virgins in California. It's a state law."

In his arms, Peggy was not the brisk, teasing girl who strode onto the tennis court with such concentrated determination. Even the very first time, when awkwardness and haste were to be expected, their lovemaking was gentle and tender. As he lay there, his lips against her throat, taking in the fragrance of her skin and the perfume of the freshly cut grass and lilac from two huge bushes that loomed above them, Benjamin knew that there was no excape and that he didn't want any escape.

"You," he said, whispering against the slender throat, "we're going to get married."

She didn't say anything for a moment and she didn't move. "You don't have to marry me," she said, "just because you raped me."

"I have to marry you," he said, "because I have to marry you."

She began to sob. "Oh, my dear, my dear, my dear," she said, holding his head so tight that his lips were crushed against her and he couldn't speak.

The colonel had no difficulty speaking, though. Benjamin was afraid that the Colonel would object to the marriage because Benjamin was Jewish. The Colonel, it turned out, was a fierce atheist, and didn't mind at all that Benjamin was Jewish. But he minded a lot of other things.

"She's too damn young," Woodham said as they sat across from each other on a hot Sunday afternoon in the library of the rambling frame house next to the Bronstein's garden. "She's only twenty."

"My mother was married before she was twenty," Benjamin said.

Woodham snorted and ran his hand the wrong way against his graying tonsure. "So was Peggy's mother," he said.

"Well?" Benjamin said.

Woodham poured a whiskey for each of them. "Women grew up quicker in those days," he said. He handed Benjamin his glass. He noticed the little smile on Benjamin's lips. "All right," he said, "they didn't. But there wasn't a war on in those days. I don't want my only daughter to be left a widow, probably with a kid, at the age of twenty-one, if you want to know the truth. Why can't you wait?"

"Because I can't wait," Benjamin said. "*She* won't be waiting when the war's over and I'll lose her."

"That's what she says, too. About you." Woodham drank his whiskey irritably. "Everybody thinks the god-damn war's going to last forever.

Maybe it'll be over in a month. Who knows?"

This was in 1942. "It won't be over in a month," Benjamin said. "You know. And I know."

"Have you got any money?" Woodham tried a new tack.

"Twenty-four dollars a month," Benjamin said.

"God damn," Woodham said. He paced annoyedly back and forth in the shaded room in front of the window. Through the window Benjamin could see the Bronstein's tennis court and the two lilac bushes.

"Why don't you wait until you get out of OCS?" Woodham said. "Then she'll at least have a second-lieutenant's pension when you get killed. I can rush through your application and—"

"I don't want to be an officer," Benjamin said.

"What's the matter, is it against your religion?" Woodham glared at him.

Benjamin laughed. "No."

"What've you got against officers?" Woodham demanded.

"Nothing. I just don't want to be one."

"Why not?"

"I don't trust myself enough," Benjamin said. "I don't want to be responsible for getting anybody else but myself killed."

"You're overeducated," Woodham said. "That's what's the matter with you. You couldn't be any worse than ninety-nine out of a hundred of the idiots they're pinning bars on every day. What's your IQ?"

"One thirty-eight."

"They grab anybody with an IQ of over one ten," Woodham said. "Especially with a college education. Don't you know that?"

"Yes, sir."

"Don't Sir me, Federov," Woodham said. "One thirty-eight! Huh! As far as intelligence goes, you're in the top five percent of the whole damned army. You don't belong as a private in the infantry. You're derelict in your duty, if you want my honest opinion." He scowled at Benjamin, waiting for a response. Benjamin sat silently, enjoying his whiskey, looking out the window at the lilac bushes.

"You're not even a good tennis player," Woodham said. "The only point that Peggy and I've agreed on since she met you is that you have a laughable backhand."

"You're both absolutely right." Benjamin stood up. He knew the argument was over. Woodham would have stopped the marriage if he could, but everybody knew he couldn't, including Woodham himself.

"If you don't get killed," Woodham said, "will you at least come out to San Francisco to live after the war, so I can see Peggy once in a while?"

"I'll try," Benjamin said.

"You can play tennis all year around. You can work on your ridiculous backhand."

They both laughed.

"Okay, PFC Federov." Woodham sighed and

they shook hands. "I wish I had eight daughters. I
wish I had so many daughters I'd have difficulty remembering their names. I wouldn't mind losing a
couple along the way then." He poured them both
fresh drinks.

They had a week's honeymoon in Atlanta, the
usual, frail wartime barricade against violence and
fear of what lay ahead in the days to come. The
ceremony in the office of a justice of the peace had
been a hasty one. Three other couples were waiting to be married. Only Peggy's father and mother
and Benjamin's platoon lieutenant and another
soldier from Benjamin's squad, a huge boy from
Kentucky who shared the pup tent with Benjamin
on maneuvers, were present. Benjamin's father
and mother hadn't been able to come down from
New York because they couldn't afford the trip,
and Louis was at an airfield in Texas.

Benjamin had sent Peggy's photograph to his
parents, and his mother had written that she was
beautiful and God bless both you children.

Woodham loaned Benjamin his car and they
drove to Atlanta over the baking roads of summertime Georgia, carefully not going more than thir-
ty-five miles an hour because of wartime fuel re-
strictions. It was not a day on which Benjamin
wanted to be stopped by a traffic cop.

They closed the yellow fake-oak door of the
meager hotel room, which was all they could find
for the seven days, and Federov locked it behind

them, hearing the steps of the bellboy who had carried up their bags retreating down the creaking corridor. They were alone in the room with the window closed and the blinds drawn against the heat of the Southern sunlight. Benjamin leaned against the door and watched his wife unpack, admiring her small, neat movements as she hung up her two extra dresses and put her things into the bottom drawers of the bureau. Neither of them said a word. There was only the silken sound of Peggy's passage across the room. When she had put all her things away, Peggy turned to him. "Give me your watch," she said, coming over to him and holding out her hand.

"It's twenty minutes past five," Benjamin said, glancing down at his wrist.

"I don't want to know the time," she said. "Give me the watch."

Benjamin gave her the watch. She put it in her bag, then locked the bag and put the key away in the drawer, under her two nightgowns. "I don't want to know the time," Peggy said, "for seven days."

They went out at odd hours, when they were hungry or wanted to swim in a pool or go to a movie, but for seven days the center of the world was a darkened hotel room with a yellow almost-oak door and one window. For seven days they forgot the tides of bleached summer uniforms that oceaned around them, forgot the snarls of command, the sound of the waiting guns. For a week life was two bodies, greedy and grateful at the

same time. Then Peggy unlocked her bag to pack
it for the trip home and she gave him back his
watch.

Two weeks later, Federov's division was moved
North. Peggy did not follow him. For one thing
they didn't have the money for the fares and rented rooms that it would have cost and they knew
that it was only a matter of a few weeks before the
division would move again, probably for overseas,
and they decided that one leave-taking was all they
could bear during that war.

Two months after his wedding day, Federov's
division was sent to England. He and Peggy didn't
see each other again for three years. They wrote
constantly, of course, but by the time Federov met
Leah in Paris, Peggy had become a remote, strange
ghost lost somewhere behind a small volume of V-
mail envelopes. He had done what most soldiers do
under similar circumstances and had had several
affairs with the locals in Cornwall, where he was
stationed for amphibious training, and with a girl
from the British Ministry of Information when he
had been sent up to London for a special liaison
course with British noncommissioned officers. He
had never felt guilty about any of the girls. His
loyalty to the ghost who sent him the dutiful V-
mail letters was suspended, postponed for the dura-
tion. A war is a long time.

Leah had been divorced in 1939 (three years too
late, she told Federov in Paris), and she liked him

and was amused to turn down the full colonels and
generals who surged after her, with the explanation that she had a date with a buck sergeant. Leah
had coquetted herself into an apartment of her
own from her elevated military connections, and
she and Federov had made love with a great deal of
satisfaction in it and Leah had talked of marriage.
The idea was attractive to Federov; he had known
Peggy for only three months or so and the ghost
behind the V-mail envelopes was a stranger, un-
real, only conventionally related to him by a hasty
and almost forgotten ceremony, a pretty faded
ghost who sent photographs of herself, like a
shipwrecked sailor casting messages in bottles into
the sea, a ghost occupied with matters that seemed
piddling and unimportant to a man fighting so
long for his life on another continent. The ghost
had no claims on him with her news of rationing,
stateside politicking in the Medical Corps, com-
plaints about the cynicism of men who hung onto
soft berths at home and who were making a good
thing of the war.

After three years the professions of love were
merely formal and dutiful. He himself sent no
photographs home. The agony of his face was no
proper adornment for the bedside table of a young
girl in a white tennis dress who went to USO
dances and sold silly books to clerks in uniform in
Georgia.

On his side, his letters were generalized, meant
to be reassuring, with no details of the massive
dying of the years 1944 and 1945 which had be-

come his daily routine. He had not known his wife long enough to tell her the truth of what he was enduring. Sometimes, when he sat down to write Peggy a letter, he had the feeling that he was writing to a friend's child, known fleetingly a long time ago, a bright, beautiful child who naturally had to be protected from the misery of the grown-up world as long as possible, a child who would grow and change so much before he saw her again that it would take a feat of memory to recognize her.

By the winter of 1945 he found it difficult to consider himself married. The years of absence outweighed too heavily the brief, interrupted months when he and Peggy had been together.

1948

HE HAD BEEN HOME FROM THE WAR FOR THREE YEARS now, but Peggy still got up and made him breakfast. He was cranky in the morning and preferred being alone to make his own breakfast and read *The New York Times*, his matutinal darkness of spirit reinforced by the morning's news from all over the world. He also liked his coffee very black, but Peggy thought it was bad for his nerves and never made it strong enough for his taste. She also thought, having been coached by her father, the doctor, that breakfast was the most important meal of the day and should include a large glass of orange juice, biscuits and jam, bacon or ham and eggs, or pancakes with sausage, a glass of milk *and* coffee. She told Benjamin and his friends that Benjamin was working too hard and was too thin and that he drank too much and ate too little, and nothing Benjamin could say, morning after morning, could dissuade her from piling the breakfast table inordinately, decorating it with their best linen and glasses and a small vase of cut flowers, and coaxing him, in the dearest way possible, to finish his food.

Peggy had the notion, too, that a wife should look her best at all times, and she had whole outfits of lounging pajamas and embroidered nightgowns and robes in which she appeared as she brought in the platter heaped with food and drink. This was the realization of the dream he had had so many bitter nights of the war. Now he had it.

All this, plus the fact that Peggy's job as a receptionist in an art gallery on Fifty-seventh Street didn't necessitate her getting out of bed until nearly ten o'clock, made it impossible for Benjamin to complain. Complaint would have been boorish and ungrateful, so Benjamin sat there, stuffing food into his mouth, furtively stealing glances at the headlines on the chair beside him, wondering daily by what ruse he could manage in the future to keep his wife in bed while he ate and drank as he pleased and grunted sardonically at the columns of *The New York Times*.

During the war, too, he had gotten into the habit of drinking a small slug of Calvados or brandy before breakfast, and this was impossible with Peggy up and about. There were also the mornings when he had a hangover. When he drank, he often became ugly and pugnacious, and Peggy's silent forbearance on the subject of the scenes of the night before made him want to strangle her as she sat across from him, sipping her cold milk like a little girl and looking like something just a little bit better than a colored photograph from *House and Garden*.

She also discussed the menus for dinner at breakfast. Surfeited with food, facing with loathing the difficulties and compromises of a young man struggling to get ahead one day more in the heartbreaking city of New York, he found it almost impossible to concentrate on such questions as, "Would you like a soufflé?" or "I saw some wonderful sea bass in the market yesterday. Are you in the mood for fish?" and, "Remember, we have to sit down for dinner at seven sharp. Prudence has to be up in Harlem by eight-thirty, the latest." Prudence was their maid, who came in at one in the afternoon and, as Peggy accurately put it, had to be up in Harlem by eight-thirty sharp each evening come what may.

It wasn't that he didn't love Peggy. He did, and often enjoyed long periods with her, and he had never gotten over his joy in her body or his appreciation of her tenderness and the amusement she gave him by her brightness and outspokenness. He just felt a good part of the time that it was too much. She *surrounded* him. She had had so many anxious, lonely years to contemplate her marriage, wondering all the time whether he was going to come back alive or not, that she had figured everything out too perfectly—the décor of the apartment, the meals she was going to serve and how they were to be served, her husband's marvelous and impossible behavior on all occasions, the people she would invite and who would invite them in return, the holidays they would take, the perfect exchange of love after the last gun had fallen silent. Benjamin sometimes felt that, in an excess of devotion, Peggy had managed to put him into a perfect vacuum in which everything was offered to him, everything allowed him, except getting out of the vacuum.

He drank, he slept with other women, he paid the bills, he felt that soon he and Louis would break through in their business, he admired the results of Peggy's loving calculation, her unswerving selflessness—but there were evenings when he walked along the avenues of New York, looking longingly at the clerks and pathetically bedecked secretaries bursting out of their ugly offices for an evening that, good or bad, had not been planned for them, and thought seriously of throwing himself under a bus because he knew he had to be home by seven o'clock. Sharp.

It was a Saturday morning. Those days, people worked on Saturday mornings. There were jonquils on the breakfast table because it was spring. The sun was shining on the plane tree, with its new pale green foliage, in the back garden of the apartment in which Benjamin and Peggy lived on East Seventy-sixth Street near Second Avenue. Looking out at the sunlit tree, Benjamin thought that the human race must be insane to inhabit cities in the springtime.

Peggy had made an apple pancake with maple syrup for breakfast. Benjamin didn't like apple pancakes, except once in a while in a German restaurant for dessert, but his usual sense of a vague, secret disloyalty to his wife kept him once more from protesting breakfast and everything that went with it. Peggy was wearing pale blue denim slacks and a white tennis shirt and her blond hair, longer now than when he had met her was caught up by a narrow black ribbon. She was barefooted. Later in the day, Benjamin knew, he would have thought the outfit delightful. If he had seen her thus for the first time that morning, he would have fallen in love with her.

"What an absolute bang of a day," Peggy said, smiling across the table at him, making sure he ate the last morsel of the apple pancake. "I'm off this afternoon. Why don't we have lunch and just wander around the city for the afternoon?"

"I have a date for lunch," Benjamin said.

"With whom?"

Benjamin always hated this question. It was part

of the vacuum, part of being surrounded. But he had never had it out with Peggy because fundamentally he believed she had the right to ask it. He never asked her with whom she had lunch. He had an exaggerated sense of the value of privacy and solitude that approached the neurotic. He also never questioned her because he was trying to give her an example, which, of course, she never followed, of the necessity of leaving as many corners as possible of one's life unexposed, even to the most loving eyes. She went through all his mail, too, and although he didn't feel she had the right to do it, whenever he called her on it she denied it and he couldn't bring himself to lay traps for her—put hairs between pages, in the fashion of melodramas, or scraps of paper, so that he could demonstrate the papers had been disarranged. As far as he was concerned, divorce was conceivable between two people who had once loved each other, or who still loved each other; detective work was not.

"With whom?" Peggy asked, the *House and Garden* loving young wife perfectly turned out for all occasions, including breakfast, interested, as a wife should be, in every aspect of her husband's life.

"Jimmy," Benjamin said. "Jimmy Foynes."

Peggy made a face, as Benjamin knew she would. Jimmy Foynes was a friend he had made during the war, a newspaperman who had stayed on and off with Benjamin's division. They had had some riotous nights together and twice had nearly been killed together, and they had both talked, in the rain and misery, of the great things they would

111

do together after the war. But Jimmy drank and was loud and spilled ashes all over the living room, never picked up a check, and appeared each time with a different girl. The girls too often answered precisely to Peggy's definition of them. Tarts, she said. The girls also sometimes made passes, with generalized affection, at Benjamin. In his own house, too. Slowly but surely, Peggy had wiped out Jimmy Foynes. Among others. Among many others. The wife keeps the address book and receives the invitations. Three years after VJ Day, Foynes never came to the apartment and, since Benjamin never went out at night without Peggy, they never had dinner together. Their friendship continued at lunches, ball games and during hurried drinks after work, before Benjamin looked apologetically at his watch and said, "I have to be home by seven."

"Can't you see him on Monday?" Peggy asked.

"He's out of town on a job," Benjamin said. "I can't get hold of him."

"All right," Peggy said, delicately pouring honey over a small piece of toast. "I'll have lunch with you both. If I'm invited."

"But you can't stand him," Benjamin said. "You always say that . . ."

"I'll stand him today," Peggy said. She put the toast and honey neatly into her mouth.

Benjamin remembered the last few times, dating back more than a year now, that he had tried to go out with Foynes and Peggy together.

"We'll all have indigestion," he said.

"I just want to be with you today," she said.

"Oh, God," Benjamin said, bent under the crushing burden of a great love.

"You don't have to say, 'Oh, God,' " Peggy said. "I'm not *forcing* you. I just thought, a day like this . . ."

"We're meeting at the Oak Room," Benjamin said. "It's only for men."

"Only for men." Peggy nodded, subtly accusing the people who ran the Oak Room of being in on the conspiracy to break up her marriage. "I understand. Have some of this honey. It's delicious."

"I don't want any honey."

"It's delicious."

"I know it's delicious. I just don't want any." Benjamin felt his stomach clamping like a python around his apple pancake.

"How about after lunch?" Peggy asked, still calm and smiling a *House and Garden* smile.

"I have a date to play tennis at Rip's."

"I have a new racquet," Peggy said, "and I'd love to try it . . ."

"Men's doubles," Benjamin said.

"Oh," Peggy said, "Men's doubles. That's *sacred*." She drawled out the "sacred."

Why do I go on with this goddamn thing? Benjamin thought. What law says I have to go on with it? He drank his coffee. It was hot and scalded his tongue. He stood up, pretending to be a normal, happy, youngish husband home from the wars, pleased with the breakfast his beautiful wife, at great sacrifice, had prepared for him. "I have to go now," he said.

"Will I ever see you again?" Peggy asked.

Some day, Benjamin thought, some scholar should really go profoundly into the manner in which the word "ever" is used by wives.

"We're invited for drinks at the Roses' this evening, aren't we?"

"Yes," she said. "I'll meet you there." He put on his jacket and picked up a leather envelope with papers in it that he had had to look over the evening before. Peggy sat there, peering down at her glass of milk. Benjamin knew what she was waiting for. He went over and kissed her. "Next Saturday," he said.

"Sure," she said. "Next Saturday."

As Benjamin went out the door, he knew Peggy would start to cry. How many of the tears would be true tears and how many private histrionics, he would never know. She probably wouldn't know, either.

At nine-thirty that morning Foynes' office called. Foynes was not going to be able to come into town in time for lunch. He would telephone on Monday. Benjamin sat looking at the phone for several moments. Then he dialed his own number. Might as well make character while I can, he thought. He would take Peggy to lunch and the weekend would be the better for it. The line was busy. He hung up. He tried again a few minutes later. The line was still busy. He was exasperated with her this time. Is that all she does all morning? *Talk?*

He looked out the window. The fine spring morning had vanished. Dark rain clouds ambushed the sky. A piece of paper whirled outside his window, a message lost on invisible tides twenty-two stories high in the turbulent air. "Help!" "I love you!" "Sell everything." The wind increased, the sky was well into Macbeth. No tennis, Benjamin thought, aside from everything else. He sat disconsolately at his desk, feeling deprived and unjustly harassed.

The phone rang a few seconds later and he answered brusquely. "Yes?"

"There's no need to bite my head off. If you feel like that I'll hang up." It was Leah, her voice amused.

"Sorry," he said. "I was wallowing in self-pity."

"It's going to rain this afternoon, you know," Leah said. "It's black as the pit from pole to pole outside my window."

"Did you call me to give me the weather report?"

Leah laughed. He had once told Leah that her laugh was dangerous and he meant exactly that. "You know me better than that," she said.

"Lunch," he said.

"One-fifteen?"

"One," he said.

He hung up, feeling better. He didn't feel guilty, either—at least for the moment. If Peggy hadn't been so busy gabbing all morning over the phone, he would have asked *her* to lunch before Leah called.

The rain started, the torrential, spring-summery black rain of New York that seems designed to wash the city clean of all its sins or sweep it into the sea before nightfall.

Benjamin regarded the rain outside his window with satisfaction. He always got an extra pleasure out of making love in New York on rainy afternoons.

It was not all pure pleasure, though. There had been the discussion with his father-in-law, for example, a few months before.

"Peggy says that you sleep with other women," Woodham said.

"Does she?" Benjamin said, keeping his voice flat. He and his father-in-law were drinking old-fashioneds at the St. Regis bar. The Woodhams were in New York for a week, on their way to Europe for a holiday. Woodham, in his straight gray suit and his tight, fierce face, looked more like a colonel than ever.

"Yes," Woodham said. "Quite a few of your friends say so, too. Ladies, mostly."

"I was a fool," Benjamin said, "to give you those two parties this week. Or I should have introduced you only to my enemies."

Woodham laughed, a short, barking laugh. His laugh was military, formidable. "Ladies talk," Woodham said. "She's right, Peggy, isn't she?"

"From time to time," Benjamin said. He was not going to lie to the admirable, upright old man.

Woodham nodded. "Aside from that," he said, "she says you're an absolutely perfect husband."

"How little she knows," Benjamin said.

They drank their old-fashioneds in silence, watching the bartenders at their icy devotions.

"Does she want a divorce?" Benjamin asked.

"No."

Benjamin wanted to run to the phone booth across the room and call Peggy and say, "I love you, I love you." But he kept his face noncommittal and jangled the ice lightly in his glass. He knew that Woodham was waiting for him to say something more and would wait an hour, without a word if necessary, for him to say it. "I try to keep it as quiet as possible," he said.

"It's never really quiet," Woodham said. "You know that."

"I suppose so."

They ordered two more old-fashioneds.

"She's an only child," Woodham said. "She's used to being cherished."

"I cherish her, Colonel. Inordinately."

Woodham nodded again. "That's what it looks like," he said. "Outside looking in." He watched the barman take away the empty glass and put the new glass down in front of him.

"Let me ask you a question, Colonel," Benjamin said. "How long have you been married?"

Woodham looked wary. "Twenty-nine years. Why?"

"When was the first time you were unfaithful to your wife?"

Woodham sighed. "One for your side," he said resignedly. He took a long swig of his drink.

"Let me ask you another question, Colonel," Benjamin said.

"Goddamnit," Woodham said, "I was sent down here to question *you*."

"Peggy lived with you all the time I was overseas," Benjamin said. "You saw her every day. Do you think she was faithful to me?"

Now Woodham didn't look like a colonel. He looked like a divisional commander. "What'd she tell you?"

"Nothing," Benjamin said. "I didn't ask her."

"What the hell are you driving at?"

"Just that it isn't so damned important," Benjamin said. "I'm not saying there aren't marriages in which both people are faithful to each other from beginning to end. I read about them, I see them in the movies, I understand sermons every Sunday are full of them, but I don't see a hell of a lot of them these days and neither do you."

"I'm a doctor," Woodham said, "I see a lot of things other people don't see."

Benjamin ignored this last weak defense.

"You asked me what I'm proving," he said. "I'm not proving anything, except maybe that I'm alive. That I'm susceptible to beauty. That I'm not all one piece. That I'm hungry and I don't know what I'm hungry for."

"At your age," Woodham said, meaning it as a reproach.

"At my age," Benjamin said. "If Peggy is waiting for your report, you tell her I'll love her all my life. But if she says she'll divorce me because I occasionally have an affair, she can go to Reno tomorrow."

"Okay," Woodham said. "The report will go through channels." He shook his head. "Damn," he said, "at least you could *try* living in San Francisco."

Replete with lunch and a bottle of wine, he climbed the steps of the converted brownstone house, behind Leah. He followed the womanly straight back, the glowing hair, the slightly swaying trim hips under the green linen dress, the long perfect legs. The hallway was dim; they mounted deliberately, decorously, savoring the knowledge, each of them, of how soon that decorum would be shattered.

They made love two or three times a week. The pleasure Leah gave him was as exquisite as in the beginning in Paris. But in his reveries, dozing before falling off to sleep or sitting in a subway car, closing his eyes to shut away the sad faces of the other travelers, the moment he relived with most intensity was the silent mounting of the steps behind the superb tall woman, looking at the elegantly tailored hips, anticipating, secretly possessing, as Leah took out her key and prepared to unlock the door to her apartment.

They lay side by side in the shadowed room. The curtains were drawn, the rain drummed outside the window, but the sun was out, too, wavering pale rays through the slit in the draperies. A bedside clock ticked softly. It was nearly five o'clock. His body felt weightless, aerated, anointed, victorious. He knew he should get up and get dressed and respectably descend the stairs, respectably appear at the Roses' cocktail party, the private treasure of the afternoon's sensuality hidden, the clue to its whereabouts a memorized telephone number. It was warm in the room and they lay naked, the sheet thrown back, Leah's skin gleaming in the rainy, filtered light of late afternoon. Another five minutes.

"What did you say?" Leah asked.

He was surprised. He hadn't realized that he had spoken. "I said, 'Another five minutes,'" he said. "Only I thought I just *thought* it."

"Love and run," Leah said, but without complaint.

"We've been here for two and a half hours."

"Gentlemen don't count," Leah said. "The truth is, I have to get up, too. There's a cocktail party that I—"

"Where?"

"Some people called the Roses."

"I'm going there, myself," he said. "I didn't know you knew them."

"I don't," Leah said. "A gentleman is taking me there. He's calling for me here in an hour."

"Busy day in the East Sixties," Benjamin said.

"Ugly man," Leah said calmly. "Your wife going to be there, too?"

"Yes."

"Good," Leah said. "Finally, I'll get a chance to meet her."

"I can't wait," Benjamin said. He remembered the scene at breakfast. It was the wrong day for this meeting. Though he couldn't imagine a *right* day. He turned his head and kissed Leah. "See you at the next drink," he said, and started to get out of bed.

Leah reached out and held him. "And now a message from our sponsor," she said.

He lay back, pleased to have an excuse not to leave that rain-enclosed room, that joyous May-time bed, for another few seconds.

"The gentleman who's coming to take me to the cocktail party," Leah said, "is a man called Stafford. Do you know him?"

"No," Benjamin said.

"He's an extraordinary man," Leah said.

Benjamin made a face.

"Don't be childish," Leah said. "Would you prefer it if I only saw ordinary men?"

"Of course," Benjamin said. "The more ordinary the better."

121

"I knew you were mean," Leah said, "but I didn't know you were *that* mean."

Benjamin sighed.

"What're you sighing about?" she said.

"You're going to say something I'd rather not hear," Benjamin said.

"I've been seeing him for three months," Leah said. "He's my *evening* feller."

"You know what the Italians say," Benjamin stroked the thick, straight hair that fell around her shoulders. "Only peasants make love at night."

"Joke," she said. She sounded suddenly bitter.

"Sorry," he said.

"He's one of the handsomest men alive," Leah went on, her voice uninflected, "and one of the smartest. And most generous. And rich, rich, rich. And he's asked me to marry him."

Benjamin lay silent for a moment. "Question," he said. "Why do you bother with a poor, domesticated, afternoon type like me at all?"

"I have my reasons, dear," Leah said.

"Are you going to marry him?"

"Yes," she said. "If."

"If what?"

"If you won't marry me."

Benjamin didn't say anything. Now that it had been said, he knew that he had been expecting it. For a long time.

"I think I've exhausted all the possibilities in being everybody's popular unmarried friend in New York," Leah said. "I want to have a home. I want to give up the damn store." She ran an antique shop on Third Avenue that her father had owned for many years and that had become one of the smartest places in New York since she had taken it over on her return from the War. "I want children," she said. "I want my own husband, not somebody else's. Do I sound hideously bourgeois?"

"Leave out the 'hideously,' " Benjamin said.

"Well, there it is." She lay still, staring up at the ceiling, carefully speaking without emotion, making no claims, allowing the splendid nude body and the startling face make all her claims for her without words.

Benjamin sat up, swung around, sat on the edge of the bed, his back to her. He saw his reflection in a wavy, dark antique mirror on the opposite wall. His body looked drowned in the gold-veined dim glass. His reflection reminded him of all the prizefighters he had see who were losing, who were battered and outgunned and exhausted and who sat on their stools wondering if they could get through the next three minutes.

"Do I have to put my vote in the box this minute?" Benjamin asked.

"No," Leah said. "I told John I'd give him an answer in a week."

"A week," Benjamin said. He stood up and began to dress. It had stopped raining. The rays of sunlight coming in through the divided curtains were steady and bright yellow now. There were splinters of gold all over the room, on the perfume bottles, on the glass of a framed print on the wall, on Leah's breasts. Benjamin dressed in silence. There was a knot in the lace of his left shoe and he said, "Damn," as he struggled with it. Leah didn't move. Golden flecks came and went in her eyes as the curtains sighed in a flicker of wind and the sun's rays shifted with the rustling cloth. This room is going to be here, Benjamin thought, she will be lying on that bed on other afternoons with the rain outside, and I won't be here. Oh, damn, damn, damn, he thought. Then he had to smile, even the way he felt at that moment. One "damn" for a shoelace and only two more for such a shipwreck of love.

He brushed his hair neatly, settled his tie into his collar. In the mirror he looked unmoved, everyday, undamaged, a young man in correct clothes, making his way up in New York, a man who knew the right places to go, the right answers to give, the right people to love. In the mirror, late on a sunny afternoon, in the changeable weather of May.

"In a week," he said, when he was dressed and ready to go. He leaned over the bed and kissed her forehead. She looked up at him, unsmiling, her eyes open. "See you in an hour or so," he said, and went out of the room, out of the apartment, and decorously down the staircase and into the noise of the traffic of the city, into the washed, brilliant evening air.

As he entered the crowded room with its mingled odors of fresh flowers, perfume, and gin, he saw Peggy's face, and he knew he was going to get drunk that night. She was standing near the windows, which looked out over the East River. She was making a cocktail-party pretense of being amused as she listened to two men and a pretty girl talking around her. But her eyes were on the door, like a radar fix, waiting for him. When she saw him, there was a peculiar effect, which Benjamin had never noticed in other women, of something closing down—a flower bunching its petals against a storm, a window being shut and a blind drawn, an animal disappearing into its den, a book being closed in such a way that you knew the reader hadn't liked the last page she had read. He waved to her, smiled. She didn't smile back. She turned and smiled to the man on her right and talked animatedly. Actress, he thought. Why the hell do I have to put up with it? He took a martini from a waiter, in no hurry to go over to his wife, and kissed the hostess and shook Larry Rose's hand and complimented him on the beauty of the female guests.

He took a good slug of the martini and started across the room. His body no longer felt weightless or victorious. Automatically he scanned the room to see who was there who could most advantageously be asked to dinner to serve as a buffer between Peggy and himself, to make Peggy postpone the fulfillment of the dark promise of her face at least until they got home.

For the moment, there were no guaranteed

buffers. He would have to wait until he saw what other guests arrived.

"Ben . . ." He felt his arm being held and transferred the martini to his other hand. It was Susan Noyes Federov, Louis' ex-wife, the first of three ex-wives his brother was to accumulate in his sentimental career. He turned and kissed her, false and friendly, on her cheek. Susan was a pretty woman with cleverly dyed chestnut hair and the dark, forlorn eyes of an Italian orphan. She had a full, tremulous mouth that even in laughter brought the word "defeat" to mind. "Ben," Susan said, "is Louis coming?"

"No," Benjamin said. "I don't think so."

"Is he happy?" Susan asked.

Benjamin considered the question. He knew what Susan meant. The field of inquiry, he knew, was narrow. Susan was not asking if Louis was happy because he was doing well in his work or because he had reached the semi-finals of a squash tournament or because he had made some money in the market or because a candidate he had voted for had won an election. When Susan asked, "Is he happy?" what she wanted to know was whether Louis was happy with the woman who had taken her place. And that was all. She also knew what answer she wanted to hear and so did Benjamin. He was not heartless enough to tell her that Louis was very happy indeed with his bride of three months. The tremulous mouth would tremble, the orphan eyes would remember the losses of a calamitous life. Benjamin shrugged. "It's hard to tell," he said.

"I talked to him last week. On the phone. You know, he refuses to see me. Even for lunch," Susan said. "Even though we have so many matters we have to talk about. I know he wants to see me. And I know who keeps him from doing it." A significant ex-wifely twitch of the soft, hurt mouth. "He sounded tense, Ben. Awfully tense. I'm worried about him. I think he ought to go to a psychiatrist. I have the name of a very good man. He should at least go and *talk* to the man. Don't you think he ought to go to a psychiatrist?"

"Maybe we all ought to go to a psychiatrist," Benjamin said. He finished his martini and reached for another off the waiter's tray. As soon as people start thinking about a divorce, he thought, they invite each other to go to a psychiatrist.

"It's *your* brother," Susan said reproachfully. "It has nothing to do with me. Any more. But you ought to take an interest. He's on the verge of cracking up."

"Is he?" Benjamin said. "I'll check."

"I don't like to say this, Ben," Susan said, holding onto his arm, "but you're a hard family. There's something very cold about both of you. You're both the same. Attractive. And cold. I suppose it's your mother's fault."

"We've told her so," Benjamin said. "Many times."

"You're just like him." She looked as though she

was going to cry before the next martini. "You'll joke about anything."

"We *are* awful, Sue," Benjamin said. "We remind each other of it every day." God, he thought, how brilliant it was of Louis to get rid of this one.

"I'm just happy I'm out of it, that's all," Susan said. "Oh—" She was looking past him, toward the door. "Here comes your Grand Passion."

Benjamin took a sip of his martini, making himself do everything slowly, then turned to see what sort of man Leah was considering marrying. But it wasn't Leah. It was a girl by the name of Joan Parkes, an extravagantly bronzed, extravagantly dark-haired, extravagantly curvy girl who dressed outlandishly, using African ornaments or dresses that looked like saris or tight-bodiced calico frocks with hippy skirts or Austrian dirndls. She was brainless, neurotic, and irresistible, at least for Benjamin, and he had pursued her for three months two years before, at a time when Leah had been away from the city. He had pursued her out of simple, straightforward, helpless lust, and he recognized from the way he felt as he saw her billow into the room that he hadn't changed appreciably since then. He had never even kissed her. He had taken her to the theatre, he had taken her to dinner, he had taken her to art galleries and concerts, he had even taken her to Virginia for a weekend, and she had never even let him kiss her. She didn't have affairs with married men, she said. This wasn't even true. He knew of at least two married men with whom she had had affairs. What was true was that she wouldn't have an affair with *him*.

"Never laid a hand on the lady," he said to Sue, to keep the record straight.

"That isn't what people say," said Sue.

"People say the earth is flat, too," Benjamin said. There was no hope of explaining his relations with Joan Parkes to his brother's ex-wife. There wasn't even much hope of explaining his relations with Joan Parkes to himself.

Still, he was pleased to see her. Almost automatically, knowing that Peggy was watching him and accumulating future points for debate, he drifted toward Joan. This evening she was dressed in yards of what looked like pink gauze to his untrained eye, and she was wearing something Mexican as jewelry in her hair. She was with an English movie actor whom Benjamin knew. The movie actor was an amusing man, full of all sorts of wild anecdotes, impossible to have a serious conversation with. As Benjamin approached the couple, making his way slowly, he decided that they were just the people to invite out to dinner with him and Peggy that night. His lack of success with Joan made him feel righteous and innocent about sitting down at the same table with her and his wife, and the movie actor could be counted upon to keep the conversation well away from domestic subjects.

He said hello to Joan, without touching her, and shook the actor's hand. "What's that in your hair?" he asked Joan.

"Don't you like it?" she said. She had a childish voice and the remnant of a lisp.

"I like it very much," Benjamin said. "I'm just curious to know what it is."

"It's an Aztec abacus, old chap," the actor said. "Surprised at your ignorance. What else does a girl wear to a cocktail party? Where on earth did you go to school?"

Both men laughed. Joan touched the decoration in her hair with dignity. "You're all the same," she said. "You want me to look like everybody else."

"You couldn't look like anybody else if you tried for a hundred years," Benjamin said.

"I don't know whether you mean that as a compliment or not," Joan said. "You've been so *hostile* recently."

"When Joan uses the word 'hostile,'" Benjamin said to the actor, "she means you haven't called her at least three times a day for the last two months."

"You've changed," Joan said accusingly. "You don't court me any more. You've become distant." She was joking, he knew, but only half-joking. She didn't want him, but she didn't want him to quit, either.

"Imagine being distant with Joan," the actor said. "In Britain it would be against the law."

"All right," Benjamin said, "I'll be less distant. You're both invited to dinner after this is over."

"You *are* dear," Joan said, touching his arm, everything in order again, the invitations steady and dependable. They arranged to signal each other when they thought they could politely leave.

Benjamin started toward the window, where Peggy was still standing, still talking animatedly to the same people. Then he saw Leah come in, accompanied by a tall, slender man with a gentle Yankee face. Every hair was in place on Leah's head, her makeup was flawless but unobtrusive, the body, naked and warm on the bed in the gold-flecked room only an hour before, now shaped coolly into a black silk dress that showed a wide oval of creamy skin at the shoulder. There was just the faintest quick hint of a smile in her eyes as they met his. He examined the man as the couple approached. Stafford, unfortunately, was one of the handsomest men alive, as Leah had promised, and the pain was compounded by the obvious air of goodness and humor on the long, thoughtful face. As Benjamin watched Stafford coming across the room toward him, lightly holding Leah's elbow, Benjamin knew that Leah had meant what she said when she had told him she was going to marry the man—if.

One week.

She introduced them to each other. Stafford's hand was dry and hard, the hand of an athlete.

"Leah tells me you're a tennis player," Stafford said. His voice went with his face and figure, mannerly, quiet, pleasant.

"I stumble around the court," Benjamin said.

"Don't believe him, John," Leah said. "He's wildly vain about his game."

Stafford laughed. "Leah's seen me play, too," he said. "She says we'd make a good match."

Benjamin glanced quickly at Leah. The glint of malice and amusement he had expected to see in her eyes was there, as expected.

"We ought to get together and play," Stafford said. "Are you free on Tuesday? Around five?"

Benjamin looked at Leah again. Tuesday, somehow, had become one of the days on which they usually made love. "I'm sure you can play on Tuesday," Leah said. "Every time I call your office on Tuesday they tell me you're out for the afternoon."

"Yes," Benjamin said. "Tuesday's fine for me."

"I'll call you Tuesday morning," Stafford said. "See what the weather's like. Leah has your number, I imagine."

"I imagine," Benjamin said. "Speak to you on Tuesday."

Finally he went over to the window. Susan was talking to Peggy now. Giving a bad rap, Benjamin thought, to all the male members of the Federov family, plus whatever relevant rancor she had left over from her divorce from Louis. As Benjamin approached his wife, he saw that Peggy was looking off to where Joan and her actor were chatting with Leah and Stafford. Peggy's face was even more firmly shut than when she first saw Benjamin enter the room.

"Good evening, dear." He kissed Peggy's cheek. Her hair smelled fresh and springlike. He loved the smell of her hair and he was surprised to realize that he could notice things like that, even when he was annoyed with her, as he was that evening.

"Did you have a good lunch?" Peggy asked.

"Uhuh."

"How was the tennis?"

"It rained," Benjamin said. "Didn't you see?"

"I was home all day," Peggy said. Her tone was as closed-in as her face.

"I was telling Peggy," Susan said, "that I thought Louis ought to go to an analyst."

That wasn't all you were telling her, dear, Benjamin thought, looking at his wife's face.

"She agrees," Susan said.

"Peggy's a fanatic believer in Freud," Benjamin said. "In reaction to her father, you know."

"You don't take me seriously," Susan said bitterly. "You never did. Don't think I don't know. And don't think part of what happened isn't your fault." She walked away, ready for tears.

"Why don't you leave that poor girl alone?" Peggy said. "She has enough to cope with as it is."

"She's a fool," Benjamin said. "And why did you tell her you agreed that Louis ought to go to an analyst?"

"Because I think he should."

"Oh, God."

"Am I supposed to ask you each time I open my mouth whether I have your approval or not?" Peggy spoke in a low voice that only he could hear, but the tone was furious. "Leave your telephone number at all times, so I can check. The number of the Oak Room, for example."

"What're you talking about?"

"You know what I'm talking about. I called.

The Winstons telephoned to see if we could have dinner with them and I wanted to see if it was all right with you. You weren't there, the headwaiter said."

Benjamin sighed. He could say that the headwaiter hadn't found him, that he *had* lunched there, but he felt perverse enough not to use the saving fib that evening. He felt put upon and unjustly treated. After all, it hadn't been his fault that he hadn't gone to the Oak Room. Foynes hadn't come into town and Peggy had been on the phone all morning, as he now remembered it, so he hadn't been able to invite her to lunch as he had wanted to. He looked away from his wife's closed face at the crowded party. Joan and her actor were moving toward him and Peggy. They were passing Leah. Stafford was at Leah's side, and so were several men in dark suits. Rooms in New York, Benjamin thought, are too damn complicated. He heard Leah's laugh, low, disturbing, cool, inviting. The invitation, he somehow felt, was aimed at him, although there were twenty other men in the room. Maybe, he thought, I'll call her tomorrow and tell her I'll marry her and move out of town and never go to another cocktail party again in all my life.

"Foynes's office called and said he couldn't make it," Benjamin said, annoyed with himself for feeling he had to explain. "I tried to get you, if you want to know the truth, to ask you for lunch, but the phone was busy."

"I bet," Peggy said.

"I don't care if you believe me or not." He felt holy and honest at being able to tell the truth and not be believed. Later on he would smile to himself ruefully at this oblique satisfaction, but right now, confronted with Peggy's blind mistrust, he gave full rein to the unaccustomed pleasure of being a misunderstood husband.

"Where *did* you have lunch?" she asked.

"Some people came in from out of town and I took them to—"

"What people?"

"You don't know them." Leah would never ask questions like this in a million years, he thought. The husband would do the interrogating in *that* family.

"I don't know anybody," Peggy said. "Little old wifey-pie, staying home, bent over the stove, day and night, never gets to know anybody."

From a foot away, Benjamin marveled, they'd look like a perfectly happy couple, the beautiful young woman, dazzlingly turned out, lovingly discussing the affairs of the day with her adoring husband. I wish I was a foot away, Benjamin thought. Or a mile away. Or in Madagascar.

"I invited Joan and her actor friend to have dinner with us," Benjamin said. In another moment the couple would have made their way through the crowd of guests and Benjamin wanted no surprises.

"Coward," Peggy said.

She knows me too damn well, Benjamin thought. Maybe it *really* is time to move on. He sighed again.

"One more sigh," Peggy said, "and you're out. And don't blind yourself with those martinis. That's your fourth."

"Third," he said.

"Fourth," she said. "I've been watching."

Gentlemen don't count, Benjamin remembered, from the warm bedroom that afternoon. Ladies shouldn't count, either. Peggy was only drinking vermouth over ice. Her abstinence gave her a moral edge over him that also served to irritate him. With deliberation, he finished his martini and took another off a waiter's tray.

"Susan had some interesting information," Peggy said, "about your friend Joan Parkes."

"I have an interesting plan," Benjamin said, working on his fourth or fifth martini, according to who was keeping score. "From now on, let's not talk to anybody who ever got divorced from anybody in my family."

"Ready to go, old boy?" the actor said, as he and Joan came up to them. "Peggy, you look smashing." He smiled at Peggy, who he knew liked him and she smiled back, hiding everything. She also smiled at Joan.

"Let's go to a nice, chic little French place," Joan said. "Just the cozy four of us. Oh, my God!"

"Watch it!" Benjamin said, but it was too late. Somehow, Peggy's hand had slipped and the whole big glass of vermouth had spilled all down the front of Joan's ruffled pink skirt, and Joan was dancing back unhappily, making small moaning sounds as the stain spread.

"I'm terribly sorry, Joan," Peggy said. She bent over helpfully with a small handkerchief to try to repair some of the damage.

"Don't touch it!" Joan wailed. "Oh, it's ruined. And it's the first time I've worn this dress."

"I don't know what happened," Peggy said. There was very little apology in her voice. "But don't worry, Joan, you go right back to where you got that dress . . ."

"Mainbocher's," Joan wept, dabbing hopelessly at the dress.

"You go right back to Mainbocher's tomorrow," Peggy said, sounding like a schoolteacher instructing a backward child, "and get exactly the same dress and send the bill to Ben's office. You don't mind, do you, Ben?"

"Delighted," Benjamin said.

"Now, shall we go to dinner?" Peggy asked, briskly.

"I'm not going out to dinner looking like *this*," Joan said, her emotion making her say *thith*. "I'm not going out anywhere. Eric, take me home."

"Yes, dear girl," the actor said. "Wise decision."

"I'm terribly sorry," Peggy said in the same tone she had used before.

"I don't think you really are," Joan said. She rushed across the room, trying to hide the stain on her skirt, which now had assumed the shape of the map of South America on the frail pink cloth. The actor looked briefly at Peggy, who was standing serenely in front of the window, beautifully framed by the lights of the river and the bridge and Queens in the gathering dusk behind her. Then the actor gave Benjamin a small, masculine, secret-language, understanding smile, shrugged, and went off to escort Joan home.

"Isn't it awful?" Peggy said. "You and I will just have to eat alone tonight. Mr. and Mrs. Federov in a cozy little twosome."

"Let's get out of here," Benjamin said. He had never hit a woman in his life and he didn't want to start now, with his wife, in front of forty of his best friends.

"I'd like another drink," Peggy said, like a little girl asking for another ice-cream soda. "Something happened to mine."

"In the restaurant," Benjamin said, and grabbed her arm hard and propelled her through the room. Peggy smiled graciously at everybody, the little girl who had had just the most wonderful time, ma'am, at the party, and they reached the door without Benjamin's having to introduce Peggy to Leah.

They walked in silence, or almost silence, through the dusk toward the restaurant. Peggy was humming a happy little almost-tune under her breath as she walked at Benjamin's side.

"Mainbocher's," she said calmly. "I bet that'll cost you at least three hundred and fifty dollars."

"That was a miserable, childish thing to do," Benjamin said.

"Accidents happen, darling," Peggy said. Her

face wasn't closed any more, but open like a happy tulip on a spring morning.

"Accidents!" Benjamin said. "Whom're you kidding?"

"You, darling." Peggy squeezed his arm affectionately. "I'm kidding you."

"Disgraceful," Benjamin said.

"Wasn't it?" Peggy said cheerfully. "Would you have preferred it if I'd challenged her to a duel?"

"I never touched her."

"That isn't what I heard," Peggy said.

"That damn fool Susan," Benjamin said.

"It's not nice to talk like that about members of your own family," Peggy said.

"I never touched her," Benjamin said. "Believe it or not."

"Oh, the poor girl."

"Do you want to know why I never touched her?" he demanded.

"Only if you're dying to tell me."

"Because she wouldn't let me. She doesn't have affairs with married men."

"Foolish girl," Peggy said. "That'll teach her." She patted Benjamin's arm. "You don't want to have anything to do with girls who won't have affairs with married men, do you, baby?" She chuckled. She looked mischievous and eighteen and wonderful. " *'I'm not going out to dinner looking like thith!'* " she said, getting Joan's voice and lisp exactly.

Benjamin stopped walking. He put back his head and laughed. He stood there on the open

street roaring with laughter. Peggy joined him and
they laughed uncontrollably, impolitely, conspira-
torially, unbreakably, together. When they
stopped laughing, he took her to dinner and they
had a fine time, talking about a million things, like
people who have just fallen in love and don't have
enough hours to get everything in.

He played tennis with Stafford on Tuesday and
they split four sets and decided to have dinner together, all of them, Leah and Stafford and Benjamin and Peggy, that night. They all liked each
other very much and, even before Stafford married
Leah, they were seeing each other two or three
times a week.

Peggy and he had gone to the quiet wedding.
Neither of them had ever spoken of his affair with
Leah, although he was sure Peggy finally knew
about it. And when, after her honeymoon, Leah
had hinted that she was prepared to continue with
the affair, Federov had made it clear it was over. It
wasn't easy. He knew there were going to be times
when he was going to regret his rectitude perhaps
more than he had ever regretted any of his sins,
but he was not going to make love to the wife of a
man who had become his friend and whom he admired so completely.

Since then, the couples had become inseparable.
There was no cynicism on either side because of
the past. Friendships have been built on worse
foundations. The four of them had gone on a trip
to Europe together, with their children; Federov

played tennis with Stafford two or three times a week; they were almost automatically on each other's guest list at parties; the two women went to galleries and the theatre together in the afternoons and worried about their children together; and it was Stafford who, in 1950, had suggested that the Federovs buy the house in the town on Long Island in which Stafford's ancestors had put up the first roof.

———— 1964 ————

A BATTER HIT A TRIPLE AND THERE WAS A LOT OF shouting in front of Leah and Federov as the batter slid into third base in a cloud of dust.

"I guess I'll see you tonight," Federov said, leaning back against the plank above them and watching with admiration the long, exquisite feet, in their open blue sandals, of the woman beside him. "I'm sure Peggy will want to go."

"Well," Leah said, "you've been warned. It could be worse than two weeks ago."

"It couldn't be," Federov said.

At the dinner party two Saturdays before, the subject of the German play *The Deputy* had come

141

up. It was causing a sensation in New York, as it had wherever it had been shown, because of its attack on Pope Pius XII for not having publicly denounced the German massacre of the Jews. One of the guests was a woman of about forty, a neighbor of the Staffords. She was wearing a disastrous green dress, a thin, plain woman with hyperthyroid eyes, whose husband somehow managed not to be there on most weekends. She was rarely invited out by any of the regular group of the resort. After one evening in her company Federov had understood why. He also understood why her husband found it necessary to stay in town most weekends. Her name was Carol-Ann Humes, née Fredericks, from Charleston, South Carolina, and while she usually was quiet and tried to please, she moved in an atmosphere of boredom as solid and palpable as cement.

But Stafford, who could not bear to see anyone he knew neglected or hurt and who made a point of taking care of social cripples—ladies who were being divorced, rude men with unpopular political convictions, *nouveau riche* couples with gaudy clothes and objectionable children—always had Mrs. Humes to all gatherings in his house. He was not a born host. It would never have occurred to him, as it did to Leah, to speculate whether any given party in his home was a success or not. In fact, the flow of people through his living room and past his table was not really considered by him in terms of what others called parties. People were his medium, his instructors, his pupils, his concern. If he knew them, they were his responsibility. He was rich in spirit as well as in worldly goods, and his hospitality was general.

In the middle of the discussion, already heated, about the German play, Mrs. Humes said that it was a shame that such a play could be put on the stage in New York. She wasn't even a Catholic, but she felt that the Pope had been a fine man and that it was disgraceful that he could be attacked in public so many years later, when he was dead and could no longer defend himself.

Peggy, who had been in the thick of the argument, turned on Mrs. Humes. "Have you seen the play?" she demanded.

"No," Mrs. Humes said. "I wouldn't degrade myself. But I've read the critics and the articles in the newspapers."

"Don't you think it might be a good idea to see something like this before you talk about it?" Peggy asked, trying to sound friendly and reasonable and not succeeding.

"No," Mrs. Humes said. "I wouldn't even care if it was a *good* play. It's the subject . . ." She waved her sunburned hands vaguely. "The world is weary of the subject, Peggy, you might as well face it."

Peggy turned to a small, hunched man down the table from her. His name was Grauheim. He was married to a teacher in the local school and worked in the town pharmacy putting together prescriptions. He had come to America in 1949, and Europe still haunted his face and tinged his speech. "Mr. Grauheim," Peggy said, "are you tired of the subject?"

Mr. Grauheim shrugged and smiled uncomfortably. "I am something of a special case, my dear lady," he said. "I would not presume to advance my opinion—"

"Speak up, Jacques," his wife said. She was a powerful wide woman with a shock of gray hair and a face like an Indian, all bones and stoicism. "Say what you believe."

"I am not tired of the subject, my dear lady," Grauheim said.

"I'm sure there are people here and there who . . . ," Mrs. Humes began.

"Tell us why you are not tired of the subject, Mr. Grauheim," Peggy said.

"Well . . ." Grauheim laughed apologetically, using only breath. "I was in a camp for three years."

"Tell Mrs. Humes about the last days," Peggy said.

Grauheim looked helplessly at his wife.

"Tell the lady," his wife said.

"They started to move us out," Grauheim said. "The Russians were approaching. We could hear the guns. They walked us for five days and five nights."

"How many men started on the march?" Peggy said, tight-lipped. Federov sat back, not daring to get involved in the argument for fear of inflaming Peggy past all polite limits in this candlelit room on a summer's evening in the peaceful seashore resort.

"There were five thousand men who started out," Grauheim said.

"How many were alive at the end?" Peggy asked, relentless.

"Four," Grauheim said tonelessly. With one syllable, the Atlantic Ocean was drained. A road in Germany led suddenly across a dining-room table in Long Island.

"Are you still weary of the subject?" Peggy said to Mrs. Humes.

"I think it should be forgotten," Mrs. Humes said. She was flushed. She had probably drunk a little too much, to fortify herself against the evening, and for once she spoke freely, "It's only painful. What good does it do to remember? I have no prejudice against the Jews. You all know how I adore Leah. I just want to warn you. I hear from so many of my friends, fine, liberal people, absolutely without prejudice, they get it from every side, that play is just stirring up old anti-Semitic feelings, feelings people didn't even realize they had any more. You have to forget *sometime*."

"You and your friends forget six million murders," Peggy said in the general, embarrassed hush. "Mr. Grauheim can't."

Peggy's vehemence made Federov uncomfortable. He himself believed in argument only when some practical purpose could be served by it. Confounding poor Mrs. Humes was hardly worth all that emotion. Foolishly, he also felt a challenge to

145

his masculinity in Peggy's fighting for him what he considered was essentially his battle. He was surprised, too, that Stafford, as host, didn't break it up, but Stafford sat back in his chair, listening, taking no part in the conversation, consciously allowing Mrs. Humes to be educated.

"Still," Mrs. Humes went on stubbornly, "I assure you it would be the best for all concerned, and especially the Jews, if the play were taken off tonight."

"What have the Jews got to do with it?" Peggy said. "The play was written by a German Lutheran."

"Even so," Mrs. Humes said, "I am just warning you about what's happening. I have sources of information that are denied to the rest of you. I haven't the faintest idea who's a Jew here and who's not, except for dear Leah, of course, but you all live in New York and you don't know what's happening in the rest of the country."

"Carol-Ann," Stafford said politely, rising, "I think we're finished here."

But, at the center of attention and unleashed for the first time since her wedding day, Mrs. Humes rushed on. "You people," she said, including Stafford and all the guests, "admire all the wrong people. You scorn Pope Pius, who saved us all from Communism, and you approve of Pope John, who *was* a Communist . . ."

"Carol-Ann, stop being a fool," Leah said sharply.

"I know you would like me to shut up," Mrs. Humes said, "but I'm speaking for your own good. And all your woolly ideas about the Negroes." Naturally, Federov thought. Here it comes. Auschwitz to Mississippi in one easy lesson.

"I've heard, I've heard. Every summer," Mrs. Humes said. "I'm from the South and I really know about Negroes. They don't really want to live next door to you. They don't like you. They don't like to be near you. They think we have a different smell from them, just the way I know they have a different smell from us."

"Carol-Ann, darling," Stafford said. He went over and kissed her lightly on the forehead. "You smell divine." Then he said with mock seriousness to the rest of the company, "But I know several Negroes who also smell divine. Lena Horne, Diahann Carroll, Josephine Baker."

"Now you're making fun of me, John," Mrs. Humes said. She turned to the other guests, who were standing, a little embarrassedly, unhappy about the scene. "I love you all," she said. "You are wonderfully interesting. You make my summers here fascinating. But I don't want to see you get hurt, any of you. No, John," she said with dignity. "I am going to bed. I'm afraid I'm too emotional for arguments. Good night, my dear, good friends." She went out of the dining room with tears in her eyes. Stafford's mother, robust and pretty, sighed heavily. She looked to her son for a sign. Stafford nodded, and his mother, with a little

147

helpless wave of good-night to her son's guests, left the table to cross the lawn with Mrs. Humes and see her safely to bed.

There was silence for a moment and then Stafford said, "There's coffee and brandy in the living room."

In the living room people began to talk about the upcoming election, and the incident of Mrs. Humes and *The Deputy* would probably have ended there, an unpleasant few minutes in the history of a long summer, if it hadn't been for Louis. He hadn't said anything while the argument had been going on, but had sat back indolently, fixing Mrs. Humes with a quizzical, lazy look all through her performance, as though he didn't quite believe that he was hearing what he was hearing and was waiting for her to laugh or to explain it was all a joke. His usual soft manners deserted him when he was confronted by unattractive women, and he could be brusque and mocking with them, especially if they combined brainlessness with lack of charm. He was staying at the Federov's that weekend, and when he and Benjamin and Peggy got home that night, he took a drink and remained downstairs when the others went up to bed.

As Federov dropped off to sleep, he heard the tapping of a typewriter downstairs and he wondered what on earth Louis could be working on at that hour of the night.

Federov found out the next morning. At his place at the breakfast table, when he came down early to eat with the children, there was an envelope beside his plate. He tore it open. There was one sheet of paper in it, neatly typed.

"From Fort Sumter to Carol-Ann Humes and Back," he read.

There was a young lady named Humes
Who was a great expert on fumes.
With one simple sniff
She could tell you the diff
Between Baptists, Frenchmen, and coons.

Federov chuckled. His children stopped talking and looked questioningly across the table at him.

"What's so funny, Dad?" Michael asked.

"A note your Uncle Louis left for me," Federov said.

"Can I read it?" Michael asked.

Federov hesitated. "It's private," he said.

"I could use a laugh or two myself," Michael said.

"It's an inside joke," Federov said firmly.

"I'm on the inside," Michael said.

"Me, too," said his daughter, spooning up corn-flakes.

"Not this much, boys and girls," Federov said. He folded the page neatly and put it into his pocket. He didn't want it to fall into anybody else's hands. The sooner last night was forgotten, the better it would be for everybody.

What he didn't know was that Louis had made two carbons of the limerick. And it wasn't until later in the week that he found out that Louis had sent one of the carbons to Stafford and the other one, incomprehensibly, to Mrs. Humes.

The week that followed was one of scandal. Everybody heard about the limerick by Tuesday, and phones rang constantly in the city and out on the Island. Mr. Humes called Louis in the office and, when he heard that Louis was not in, asked to speak to Benjamin.

"You tell your goddam brother," Humes said, "that unless he apologizes to my wife, I'm going to punch him in the nose the next time I see him."

Benjamin knew Louis too well to expect that Louis would apologize. He told Humes as much, then added, for Humes's sake, "The next time you describe my brother, leave out the goddams. And let me advise you that it would be unwise to try to punch him in the nose. He'll kill you." He hung up, refraining from pointing out that if Humes could only tolerate spending the weekends with his wife, he might be able to keep her mouth shut with happy results for them all.

"What the hell did you do it for?" he asked Louis when Louis came into the office and listened, grinning, to the report of the conversation with Humes.

Louis shrugged. "She's so all-out ugly," Louis said, "and she made poor old Grauheim so unhappy. A little lesson like this might do her some good. Wouldn't it be *marvelous* if the sonofabitch tried to hit me?"

Humes didn't try to hit Louis, but he did make a formal call on Stafford and told Stafford that he would not come to the Stafford house when Louis Federov was invited.

All in all, it was a banner week on the Island, and one that would be long remembered.

Leah, sitting on the bench beside him, winced as she watched her son strike out on three straight balls.

"Louis shouldn't have sent that thing to the poor woman," Federov said. "I hope he called you and John, at least, and apologized to you."

"Don't be absurd," Leah said. "John lapped it up. He had it mimeographed in the office and he's sending copies out all over the country. He's crazy about Louis." She looked maliciously at Federov. "Maybe I picked the wrong member of the family," she said.

"Maybe you did, lady," Federov said. "Maybe you did."

1936

IT WAS WHEN HE WAS GOING TO VISIT LEAH AND HER new husband, Franklin Ross, who was a friend of Federov's that Federov sailed on the Fall River

Line for the last time. He was going to Truro, on Cape Cod, to stay with the Rosses, who had rented a house there for the summer, and he went on board the steamer *Priscilla,* with a secondhand Ford he had just bought, the first automobile he had ever owned. He was working as an engineer for a construction company, and this was his first holiday since his graduation from college.

After he had put his bag into his stateroom (he had a baseball glove packed in, he remembered Eddie Roush and the smell of neat's-foot oil and New York passing by the open porthole) he went up on deck, just as the ship was pulling away from the pier. Two children, aged about four and seven, in identical navy-blue suits with knee pants, passed him on the steps. The older one looked very much as Louis had looked at the same age.

Federov was glancing back at them and nearly bumped into a young woman as he went through a doorway.

"Excuse me," he said, standing back to let her pass. "I wasn't watching where I was going."

"It's nothing," the woman said. "There is no harm done," She spoke with a bit of an accent. For the moment he couldn't place it. Middle Europe. She held the door open for him, smiling. There was a hint of coquetry in the smile and the excessively polite moment at the door. She was blond and pretty, buxom, dressed simply in a navy-blue skirt and lighter blue sweater. When he went through the door he turned to examine her. She was slowly going down the stairs, looking back at him. They both laughed.

Later, lady, Federov thought, liking the idea.

He saw her again after dinner. She was still wearing the same clothes. Federov was standing against the rail, enjoying the summer wind of the ship's passage and the lights of the Connecticut coast across the dark water. The girl was walking along the deck. She stopped a few feet away from him and leaned against the rail, too, and looked across at Connecticut, her blond hair blowing gently around the soft fair face that was going to be fat and gross later on, but was pretty and desirable now.

"Good evening," Federov said.

"Good evening," the girl said with that slight thickness of accent.

Federov moved toward her. They began to talk. Banalities. The beauty of the night. The calmness of the sea. The impressiveness of the sunset that evening. Their destinations. Truro, Nantucket. Her name. Gretchen Something. She lived in New York, she said, on West Ninety-sixth Street. They started to walk slowly along the deck. She took his arm. Slight pressure of fingers.

She had been born in Germany, she said. Essen. Explanation of accent. She had been in the United States three years.

"Oh," Federov said. "To escape Hitler . . ."

The girl stopped walking. Her tone was almost harsh. "Why should I want to escape Hitler?" she said. "I am a German."

Federov didn't want to push it. It was too beautiful a night to discuss Hitler. "I just thought—well—" he said, "a lot of people have left Germany since he got in and I thought that maybe—"

"There is no reason to leave," she said. "My family is there. My brothers. They write me. I know. I came to America to learn English, earn money. That is all."

They walked in silence. Still the slight, inviting pressure of fingers.

"It is the New York newspapers," the girl said. She wouldn't leave it alone. There was the tone of aggrievement in the not unmusical voice, a permanent grudge, a whine of persecution. "They print only lies. Nobody in New York can ever know the truth. I know. I get letters from my brothers every week. It is a young man's country now, they tell me. They can be proud again, the young men."

"Uh-huh," Federov said. No use in arguing. As he walked on the dark deck, with the smell of the gardens of Connecticut in his nostrils and the inviting touch of the soft fingers making him want to take her down to his cabin into his bed, he knew that sooner or later he would be in Europe with a gun in his hand, fighting the proud young brothers of the desirable girl at his side. But he didn't want to talk about it. Sex now, tenderness now, youth now. War later.

Another subject. Fast. "You said you work in New York. What are you—a nurse, governess?"

She took her hand off his arm and stopped walking. "Why did you say that?" she asked.

154

"Oh, I don't know. A guess. Maybe because I saw those two nice little boys a minute before I saw you in the doorway before dinner."

"People from New York are all the same." Her voice was shrill now. "If you have a little German accent, immediately you are a servant."

"There's nothing wrong with being a nurse," Federov said. "Some of my best friends are nurses." Weak joke. "You can nurse me any time you want."

"It is not funny, that, not funny at all," the girl said. Her face was closed and bitter. The fat woman, the gross *hausfrau* who was going to be there ten years later, appeared suddenly. "Yes, I am a nurse. For the two little snotnoses. I will now wish you good-night. I am not good enough to associate with New York gentlemen like you."

She turned and disappeared.

Federov slept alone and badly that night. The entire vacation was a waste of time. It rained almost every day, and his friend Ross and Leah, the new bride, argued with each other for the whole two weeks and Federov knew that a divorce was only a matter of time.

At the end of the holiday, as he drove toward New York alone in his car, he was a little ashamed because he knew he wanted to be in the same city with Leah the day the decree became final. Some ten years later, in Paris during the war, when he saw Leah in her Red Cross uniform, he knew he had been right in wanting to be in the same city with her. Only he hadn't been ashamed in Paris.

He was ten years older and he had been through a war and there were so many other things to be ashamed of by then.

———————— 1964 ————————

THE GAME WAS DRAWING TO A CLOSE. THE SUN WAS low, the shadows long on the field, the players moved in a summer's-end golden trance; his own son floated in a soft haze far away; the sound of surf came to his ears or he suddenly realized he had been hearing it all the afternoon without recognizing it, the puissant cadence of Ocean behind distant oaks two hundred years old; the beautiful, copper-haired woman, now silent beside him, was his good friend when she might very well have been among his bitterest enemies; his tall son glided like a stranger, ageless, a memory, across the green grass; his own father for a moment or two in a vanished September was alive . . .

1927

"ISRAEL, ISRAEL," HIS FATHER WAS SHOUTING DOWN-
stairs in the living room of the comfortable two-
story house in Harrison, "my name is Israel and I
want you to get that man out of my house."

Benjamin had never heard his father shout before. He was a short, sweet-tempered man, with a
naive belief in the goodness of his fellowman, an
overflow of forgiveness when that belief was
proved ill-founded.

"Israel, Israel," his father was shouting, and
Benjamin went quietly down the steps and peered
into the living room to see what was going on. His
father was there in his American Legion uniform,
and Benjamin's mother and his father's sister, Bertha, and Bertha's husband, George. George had a
bandage around his head. He was powerfully
built, about thirty years old, prematurely bald,
with a broken nose and large, rough, workman's
hands.

"Sssh, Sssh," Benjamin's mother was saying.
"The children . . ."

"Let the children hear!" Israel Federov said.

"Let them know about this thug." He turned on George. "You go out and you go to Boston and you demonstrate, you make a nuisance of yourself, you disturb the peace, you yell, 'Everybody is wrong, the Governor, the judge, the president of Harvard University, highly respected men, Americans!' And who is right? Two Italians who throw bombs. And you get hit on the head by a policeman! This is America, not Russia! And ten days in jail. Ten *years* it should have been."

"Sssh . . . ," Benjamin's mother said, "the children . . ."

"And you have the gall to come to this house with my sister," Israel shouted, ignoring his wife for the first time in fifteen years of marriage, "and ask for pity. You have no job, your boss doesn't like jailbirds. What a surprise! You have no money, you spent all your money going to Boston to make trouble, a veteran of the United States Army should strip himself to the bone to support a bum, a man who fights with policemen, a man who thinks it's the right thing to do in America to kill important men, to throw bombs, to call the president of Harvard a liar."

"Israel . . . please . . . ," Benjamin's mother said softly.

"That's it," Benjamin's father said. "Israel. I go to the American Legion meeting, Israel Federov American Expeditionary Force. Corporal Israel Federov, born in Russia, a Jew, and what do they say at the meeting? I'll tell you what they say. They say, 'Jews are troublemakers, they are anarchists, they should be thrown out of the country.' And if I say, 'No, Jews are not like that, they are patriots, I was hit by the machine gun in France, I laid in the mud bleeding a day and a night,' they say, 'Maybe, but what about your brother-in-law George in jail in Boston for two Italians?' "

Standing unnoticed on the steps outside the living-room door, Benjamin knew his father was right. If he could have, he would have gladly dragged his Uncle George out of the house with his bare hands.

"Jew, Jew," George said. He had a rough outdoor voice to go with his broken nose and his workman's hands. He had been a day laborer and a longshoreman, and his last job had been as a truck driver for a furniture-moving company. "Why don't you forget Jew for a minute?"

"Forget," Israel shouted. "*You* forget. Me, I remember. In Russia, they came into the villages and they said, 'I'll take that Jidok'—and they tore a boy of sixteen from the arms of his mother and they put him in the army of the Czar for twenty-five years. Degradation, abuse, Siberia, a lifetime. Die."

"They got no army of the Czar any more," George said. "Finally, they got a decent government."

"Decent," Israel said. "Hah! Worse. Don't tell me. I know the Russians."

"Israel, please . . . ," Benjamin's mother said.

Israel disregarded her and went up close to George, who towered over him. "When they ask me tonight at the Legion, 'What about your Jew jailbird brother-in-law up in Boston?' what should I tell them?"

"Tell them I'm not a Jew," George said. "I'm an American. I was born in Cincinnati."

"Why don't we all sit down and have a cup of tea," Benjamin's mother said, "and not get so excited?"

"Cincinnati!" Israel said. "Don't make me laugh. All they'll remember is Jew. Get out. Bertha, get that bum out of my house."

"Come on, Bertha," George said. Even to Benjamin he sounded tired and beaten. "There's no hope here." He turned to Israel. "In the future things will happen and you will remember this day and you will say to yourself, 'That bum George was right to get hit on the head by a policeman. I should've cried my tears, too, for the two Italians.' "

George and Bertha saw Benjamin as he stood there at the foot of the stairs, but they said nothing to him as they went out of his father's house for the last time.

Israel Federov, aged six, had passed through Ellis Island on the long voyage from Kiev by way of Hamburg, and was made into an American in the slums of New York City, in vacant lots along the East River where they played with taped baseballs, homemade bats, and without gloves. Israel Federov was made into an American catching behind the plate bare-handed in the years between 1895 and 1910. Israel Federov was an American with an old catcher's hands, with three broken fingers, who, even when he was forty-five, was still nimble on wild pitches and could throw out fleet young runners who tried to steal second base on him.

Israel Federov had accompanied his son Benjamin to Pennsylvania Station in 1942 and had tried to carry Benjamin's barracks bag, because it was the end of Benjamin's overnight pass and he was going down to Newport News to embark for the war. Louis was already overseas in the Air Force. Benjamin didn't allow his father to carry the bag.

"I'm not an old man yet," Israel said, but he didn't make a point of it. "Myself," he said as they went through the uniforms and clasped couples of farewell, "myself, I left from Hoboken in 1917."

There never had been any question about the Federov sons avoiding the Army after Pearl Harbor. For Israel Federov, if there was a war and you were a young man, you fought it. Standing in the gray light of the station, with the massed murmur of good-bys making a different music from the drums that had marched Israel off to his war, Benjamin remembered the legend, now a fixture in the family history, of his father's rage against his brother Samuel, the pianist, who had planned to have himself ruptured to avoid the draft. Recalling various accounts of the scene, which had taken place when he was little more than an infant, made

161

Benjamin smile, even at that moment, when sixty seconds more would separate father and son, perhaps for years, perhaps forever.

Later on, when he had his leave in Paris, he had wandered into the Hotel Crillon, on the Place de la Concorde and had smiled again, thinking of his father, as he read the quotation from the letter of Henry IV to the nobleman whose name now was memorialized by the hotel.

"Pends-toi," the quotation, in large gilt letters on the wall, had read, *"brave Crillon. Nous avons combattu à Arques et tu n'y étais pas."* With the help of a pocket dictionary, Federov had made the translation: "Hang yourself, good Crillon. Today we fought at Arques and you were not there."

Samuel, the almost-ruptured pianist, could hardly be confused with the Duc de Crillon, and Israel, a small, poverty-worn Russian immigrant among the uniforms in Pennsylvania Station in 1942, bore little outward resemblance to Henry IV. But in another language and in perhaps somewhat different terms, Israel had made much the same statement to his pianist brother.

"Hoboken," Israel said. "The band played as we sailed out of the harbor. And I came back." This was said with something related to a smile, but Benjamin understood that he was being ordered, as obliquely as possible, so as not openly to offend God in his mysterious decrees, to follow in his father's footsteps and return. Israel was trying so hard to be an American veteran, an American father, that he almost succeeded in not weeping when he put his arms around his son and said good-by.

—————————— **1957** ——————————

AS HE WAS DRESSING, BENJAMIN HEARD HIS FATHER playing on Michael's toy electric organ downstairs in the living room.

Although Israel couldn't read music, he had played the piano by ear all his life, in a banging carefree style. Michael, six years old, was listening. Benjamin was taking the old man (frail now after a lifetime of work and two heart attacks and nothing left of the nimble, bare-handed catcher) to Yankee Stadium to see the Yankees play Detroit. Israel was picking out the "Star Spangled Banner" on the toy when Benjamin came into the room. "My fingers still work," Israel said as he played the last notes, tremolo. He was freshly shaven, his skin pink and healthy-looking, and he was wearing a neat, blue-figured bow tie, like President Truman. His clothes hung terribly loosely on him and he stood up slowly. He leaned over and kissed Mi-

chael on the head. "Never be a catcher," he said.
"It's terrible for the legs." He gave Michael a
dime. "Tell your mother to buy you an ice-cream
cone."

He and Benjamin got into a cab and started toward Yankee Stadium. They were on Lenox Avenue and 138th Street, driving up the broad street,
with the Negroes leaning against the storefronts
enjoying the May sunlight, and Israel was saying,
"The best catchers I ever saw were Bill Dickey and
Al Lopez. I never saw a catcher back up first as fast
as Al Lopez when he first played for Brooklyn
in . . ."

And then he died.

His father lay in the coffin in a large flower-
banked room in a funeral chapel on Columbus Avenue in New York. Benjamin was the first one into
the room, holding his mother's arm, with Louis behind him, after the undertakers had prepared Israel for burial and set the scene.

Irresistibly, he was drawn to the coffin, and he
left his mother with Louis and strode rapidly
across the long room and bent down and kissed his
father's forehead. It was as cold as marble, but still
Federov had an instinctive moment of surprise
that his father didn't move or smile with pleasure
as he had always done, as far back as Federov could
remember, when he saw his son.

Federov had been too distracted by the bustle of
making the funeral arrangements to forbid the undertakers to use cosmetics, and now Israel Federov

was going to have to travel through eternity with rouge and powder on his still face and lipstick on the mouth that had always been so kindly in life and now was pulled down by death into severity, like the histrionic scowling mouths of generals during the war who wanted to look tough and heroic for the photographers.

Israel Federov had been heroic in his way, maybe more so than the generals, but the heroism had come from the endurance of a world that had battered at him with a thousand small, ugly blows that no photographer would have had any interest in recording.

As he looked down at his father, Federov thought, I never even asked him the name of the town in which he was born.

Then he moved away from the coffin so that his mother and brother could say their own farewells, his mother weeping, Louis pale but controlled. God damn those miserable undertakers, Federov said to himself, walking away from the coffin. It served to keep him from crying. Nobody was going to see him cry. He was going to cry for his father, but later, at curious, unexpected moments, for years to come, perhaps for the rest of his life, but always alone and behind locked doors or in a place where nobody would know him or notice him or be interested in his grief.

The relatives, the uncles and aunts and cousins who had populated his youth and whom he had all but forgotten in the years between and whom he had difficulty now in recognizing in their present disguises of maturity and old age, shook his hand, kissed him, murmured consolation. He was involved, he thought, in the rites of strangers, whose voices had emerged, for this one day, out of the hush of antiquity.

"Tell me what your father was like," the rabbi said. They were in the living room of his parents' apartment on Riverside Drive, before the funeral. The rabbi was to conduct the service and deliver the eulogy. The rabbi had never known Israel. He was young and brisk and professionally sympathetic, and Federov was sure that as soon as he left the apartment, he would jot down some hurried, businesslike notes for the speech the next morning.

Federov knew that the rabbi wanted to hear that Israel had been a true believer, had prayed with shawl and philacteries every morning, had fasted on Yom Kippur and never missed the Passover *seder*. None of this was true. Israel had been a Jew, *that* was true; he had been proud of Jews who made names for themselves in the Gentile world and had despised Jews whose actions had reflected badly on their people; but he had rarely gone to synagogue and had been too modest to believe that God took any interest in him whatever.

"What was my father like?" Federov repeated. He shrugged. Who could answer a question like that? "He was a good catcher," he said.

The rabbi smiled. He was a Reformed rabbi and he smiled to show that he could bear his religion in a modern manner when necessary.

"What else?" Federov shrugged again. "He was a failure, he was poor, he worked like a slave, he never said no to me. Even when he came home from work exhausted on a spring evening he would go out to the vacant lot near our house and hit flies to me until it got dark. He never hurt anybody, he had a foolish belief that people were good, he loved his wife, he went to war, he saw me off to war, he did what he could." Federov stood up. "I'm sorry, Rabbi," he said. "Ask somebody else what my father was like. Just make your speech short and simple and go easy on the emotion tomorrow, if you don't mind."

Then he went out of the apartment to a bar nearby and had two whiskeys.

The rabbi nearly followed instructions. The speech was only ten minutes longer than was absolutely necessary and he didn't try too hard to draw tears, and Federov felt he earned the hundred dollars Federov was going to give him that afternoon.

At the grave in New Jersey, where the new pile of earth that was to cover the coffin was covered with a tactful green tarpaulin to keep the evidence of ultimate clay from the mourners, Federov and his brother Louis had to recite the prayer for the dead as the coffin was lowered. Neither of them knew Hebrew and they had tried to memorize the prayer from a pamphlet that had it printed in phonetic English. It was like boning up for an exam. But when the moment came, Federov could only remember bits and pieces of the lament and was embarrassed by the quick way the other eight mourners, who made up the *minyan* of ten, as prescribed by the Law, rushed in to cover his ignorance. Christ, he thought, what kind of a Jew am I? It is all ridiculous. I don't believe a word of it. He's dead and gone and this is merely theatre.

As long as it was only theatre, it would have been better to bury him at Arlington with the other dead soldiers.

When I go, Federov thought, as he mumbled the incomprehensible lament of his ancestors, I am going to be cremated. Privately. Without a word. Let them dump my ashes anywhere. On the places I have been happy—on the grass of a baseball field in Vermont; in the first bed in the city of New York where two virgins made love; on the balcony overlooking the roofs of Paris where a sergeant on leave had stood in the evening during the war with a beautiful redheaded American girl at his side; in the cradle of his son; in the long waves of the Atlantic in which he had swum so many sunny summers; in the dear and gentle hands of his wife . . .

Or in the places where I have been unhappy or in danger. In the kitchen of a country club in Pennsylvania; in an old Irishwoman's apron pocket; on the wide curving steps up which a drunken girl in a white dress had mounted twice in one night; on the farmhouse outside Coutances where a shell had hit ten yards from him and had not exploded; at Dachau, which he had made himself visit; at Camp Canoga, where, in dying, two Italians he had never seen had brought him the shock of being an outsider and alone.

The prayer droned on by the side of the open grave. By a quirk, the prayer he had learned just the day before was forgotten and another one, which he had read many years ago in a travel magazine, in an article about Jerusalem, came back to him. It was the prayer recited before the Wailing Wall, and it came back to him with total clarity, as though he had the glossy page before him

> For the Temple that is destroyed . . .
> *We sit in solitude and mourn.*
> For the walls that are overthrown . . .
> *We sit in solitude and mourn.*
> For our majesty that is departed . . .
> *We sit in solitude and mourn.*
> For our great men who lie dead . . .
> *We sit in solitude and mourn.*
> For the precious stones that are burned . . .
> *We sit in solitude and mourn.*
> For the priests that have stumbled . . .
> *We sit in solitude and mourn.*
> For our kings who have despised Him . . .
> *We sit in solitude and mourn.*

At a sign from the rabbi, he dropped the carnation he had been given onto his father's coffin. One by one, the others did the same. He helped his mother to the car, with Louis on the other side. The cortege started toward the city. Federov took a last look back. The grave-diggers were taking the tarpaulin off the pile of brown earth. I should have given them a tip, Federov thought. Maybe then they'd have waited until we were out of the gate.

—————————— **1964** ——————————

IT WAS THE LAST INNING, AND FEDEROV WAS THIRSTY after having sat in the sun all afternoon. As Michael passed him going out toward center field, Michael greeted Leah.

"Good afternoon, Mrs. Stafford," he said, minding his manners.

"Hello, champ," Leah said.

"I'll be in Vinnie's bar," Federov said to his son. "Come on over when the game's finished and I'll drive you home."

"Ok, Daddy-o," Michael said, and trotted out to his position in center field.

Federov turned to Leah, still sitting, propped on her elbows, her long legs slanted down to the bench below her, the brim of her straw hat throwing a deep shadow over the top half of her face.

"Like a beer?" Federov asked.

"No, thanks," she said.

"Aren't you thirsty?"

"Uhuh."

"But no beer?"

"Not with you."

"Why not?"

"The town's too small," Leah said, smiling; getting even, consciously perhaps, or unconsciously, Federov thought, for the rejection of 1947. Leah had a long memory and that was the only occasion in her life she hadn't held a man she wanted, and from time to time, when they were alone, she made Federov pay for that singular defeat.

"I'm a respectable matron now," she said. "Haven't you heard?"

Federov stood up and looked down at her.

"No," he said, "I hadn't heard."

She tilted her head back. The green eyes mocked him.

"You're too goddam beautiful," he said, "I'm waiting for the day you begin to fade."

"You should live that long, boychek," she said, for one second Leah Levinson from the Bronx.

"See you tonight," he said.

"At your own risk." She watched him as he passed behind home plate and across the street to his car.

The beer tasted wonderful, and Federov drank the first one down quickly in the dark, empty bar. He ordered another one and nursed it, waiting for his son.

The television set was on, a baseball game, the Yankees playing the Red Sox up in Boston. Federov watched idly for a while, amused at the

171

difference between what he was watching on the screen and what he had seen all afternoon on the high school field.

"Do you think they'll win the pennant?" he asked Vinnie, the bartender.

"They always do," Vinnie said. "The bastards."

Federov smiled at this automatic hatred of otherwise sensible men for permanent winners. He decided that, when he got to his office, he'd ask his secretary to get a pair of seats for Michael and himself for all the home World Series games as soon as they went on sale. He enjoyed taking his son to games, mostly because of Michael's attempt to be cool and critical of what was happening on the field, wanting, in this atmosphere of men, to be more adult than any of them, only to whoop with childish glee when his idol of the moment hit a home run or made a backhand catch of a line drive. It made Federov more tolerant of the masks he himself put on and the ease with which they were broken.

Federov had taken Michael to his first big-league game when Michael was six. The Giants were playing the Reds at the Polo Grounds. The Yankees were a more interesting team to watch, but it was at the Polo Grounds that Benjamin, aged six, had watched *his* first baseball game, at his father's side. An uprooted people, Federov had thought half-mockingly, we must make our family traditions with the material at hand. There was no ancestral keep to bring the male heir to; no hallowed family ceremonies into which to initiate a son; no church or synagogue or cult you believe in so that your son and his son after that could attach themselves automatically to three millennia of myth, no broad acres that had been lovingly tended for hundreds of years by people of the same blood and name to walk across with a six-year-old boy. He could not take his son to the spot where his father had gone bankrupt in the hardware business in 1927 and say, "Here your ancestors, while dying, preserved their honor." He could not take his son to Russia and seek out the town where his grandfather or his own father had been born and read a plaque on the side of a building commemorating either event. He didn't even know the name of the town and whether or not the Germans had left it standing. He couldn't even take his son to the place in Newark where he, Benjamin Federov, had been born, because the family had moved four months later and he didn't know the name of the street and had never thought of asking. He had been born on a kitchen table, his mother had said, but he doubted that at this late date the table could be found so that his son could offer sacrifices upon it. So, bereft of other tribal paraphernalia, he took his son to the Polo Grounds, because when *he* was six *his* father had taken him to the Polo Grounds.

In those years, just after the First War, both the Yankees and the Giants used the field, and it was the Yankees he had seen that first day with Israel. He didn't remember much of what he had seen

that afternoon and had been more interested in
the frankfurters and sarsaparilla his father had
bought him than in the game itself, but his father
had kept the scorecard for years and much later, in
cleaning out an attic, Federov had found the crum-
bling, yellow card. It had been carefully marked
by his father, with runs, hits, errors, singles, outs,
shortstop to first base, strikeouts, substitutions, all
the elaborate, finicking code of the game, to remind men on winter nights of great deeds done on
summer afternoons. Scanning the brittle scrap of
yellowed paper, preserved from his childhood, Federov had realized he had seen heroes that day—
Babe Ruth in right field, Home-Run Baker at
third, Peckinpaugh at first, Waite Hoyt, the Flat-
bush undertaker, on the mound. The Yankees had
won then, too, Federov remembered.

Nobody played baseball in the Polo Grounds
any more, and they were tearing it down to put up
blocks of apartment buildings.

There were other traditions, of course, that his
son might be induced to share. Going to war, for
example, and seeing a son off to war, as his father
had done. All within the span of less than twenty-
five years. Michael was thirteen. Within eleven or
twelve years, the ritual might very well be repeated. Three generations of the men of the same family sailing to battle would make quite a respectable,
almost ancient, tradition in a country as young as
America.

Pilgrimages to battlefields on which your forbears had distinguished themselves was also something that might be built up, with a little application, into a tradition, although he had neglected to visit the Argonne, where his father had fought, and when in London with his wife and son in 1960 he had not sought out the building on Pall-Mall where he had made love to a skinny girl from the British Information Service when a bomb fell on a building three doors down. Although he was not in as overt a military position at that moment as a captain of infantry leading a charge, if he had been hit by the bomb fragment that had broken the window of the bedroom in which he and the girl were lying, he would have been awarded a Purple Heart for being wounded in combat. So, technically, it had been a battlefield, and in his own way he had been fighting on it.

He hadn't gone down to the beach where he had landed, either, because it was raining that week, and he hadn't shown his son the cemetery where his platoon lieutenant was buried, because they were there for a holiday and Peggy thought children got used to the idea of death soon enough, anyway. The towns he had been among the first to enter in 1944 were of no historical significance and were off the tourists' beaten track, and it was much more enjoyable to spend the time swimming off the rocks at Antibes. Leah Stafford and her husband and children were with them on the trip, so they could hardly be expected to make a sentimental expedition to the top-floor apartment behind the Place Palais Bourbon where Leah and he had lived together on his week's leave. There went another tradition.

There was a roar from the television set and Federov looked up. A Yankee batter had hit a long fly to left field and it bounced off the fence and the Boston left fielder misplayed it and let it get away from him, and by the time it came into the infield the Yankee was standing on third base.

"The error sign is up," the announcer's voice said. "The official scorer is calling it an error."

Error, Federov thought. Error. The reward of so much human endeavor. The fielder had run as fast as he could, had used his talents, his experience, his nerve, to the utmost, and in the end the error sign had gone up.

He watched the left fielder walking, dejected, his head down, back to his position, and thought of his own son roaming an almost equally exposed outfield, because all games are played in naked arenas where exposure to judgment is constant, even a bumpy high school field on a lazy Saturday afternoon, with only the players and a handful of spectators to say, aloud or in silence, Thumbs up or Thumbs down.

He knew that his son's team was ahead by one run and he hoped that if anything came Michael's way in center field he'd hold onto it. His thoughts now on the dark side of men's adventures on playing fields, Federov remembered the misjudged

fly at Camp Canoga that had cost the game and
Bryant saying, "And you're not in the lineup tomorrow, either. You're a jinx, Federov."

1946

FEDEROV HAD SEEN BRYANT ONLY ONCE SINCE THEN.
It was just after the war and it was in a half-empty
subway car going uptown, and Bryant was sitting
alone, wearing a dark coat with a velvet collar and
a derby hat, like a Tammany alderman or the vice-
president of a small American bank who had been
befriended by the wrong people on a short visit to
London. With all that, Bryant looked surprisingly
young and in good shape. For a moment Federov
hesitated about going over, but was ashamed of
himself immediately and stood up and walked
across the car and said, "Hello, Dave."

Bryant looked up at him, unrecognizingly. His
eyes were dull and bloodshot. There was a smell of
liquor on his breath. "Hello," he said.

"I'm Benjamin Federov," Federov said. "From
camp."

"Oh, sure, hiya, Ben." Bryant stood up and put
out his hand. The second handshake, Federov

thought. "Sure, sure, I remember," Bryant said. "Good old Tris. Tris Speaker." He smiled his own congratulations to himself for the accuracy of his memory.

Federov had a few more stations to go and they talked of the old days of 1927. "That boy Cohn," Bryant said naturally. It was a cinch he wouldn't have failed to recognize Cohn, even fifty years later. "An exceptional human being," Bryant said portentously. "Exceptional. It's a shame what happened to him."

"What happened to him?" Federov asked.

"You mean to say that you didn't hear?" Bryant asked, incredulous that anyone who had ever known Cohn would be ignorant of the least action of that hero.

"No," Federov said. "I never heard anything about him since that summer."

"Amazing," Bryant said. "I thought everybody knew. He got killed during the war. In 1940."

"1940?" Federov said. "We didn't get into the war until '41."

"He joined the RAF. He flew his own plane, you know," Bryant said.

"No, I didn't know."

"Uhuh. I flew with him a lot. Weekends. Holidays. All over the place. Lake George. Down to his uncle's place in Key West. God, we had times. I tell you. The day the war broke out he went up to Canada and enlisted in the RAF. You know Cohn. He couldn't stay out of anything. He was killed over London."

They stood in silence for a moment, remembering Cohn. Now that Bryant had told him, what Cohn had done seemed inevitable to Federov, fated. With Cohn's character, which must have only been intensified with the years, the war must have seemed just another athletic event in which he could excel without exertion, another *Bye, Bye, Bonnie,* another holiday in a new town.

"God, he was clever," Bryant said. "Remember that song he made up—that Sacco-Vanzetti thing" —Bryant began to hum, searching for the words. "God, he was full of laughs. An all-'round boy. A real all-'round boy. How did the beginning go again? I don't remember, do you?"

"No," Federov said. He was sorry he had come over to say hello. He didn't want to hear any more about Cohn. "I was in England during the war, too," he said, just to switch the subject.

"Were you?" Bryant said without interest.

"How about you?" Federov asked. "Where were you?"

"In Washington," Bryant said gravely, in the tone that strong and taciturn men use in speaking of sacrifices they have made and dangers they have survived.

Federov managed not to smile. Bryant, he thought, you're a born, irrevocable, third-string man. "Sorry," he said, "here's my station." He hurried out, making a pretense of being afraid of having the doors close on him, so that there would never be a third handshake . . .

Why, when it's two out and I'm pitching, the clever, persuasive voice argued out of the cool blue mountain dusk, *and the ball's hit out toward center field, I don't even look around, no matter where it's going. I just throw away my glove and start walking toward the bench because I know Benny's out there, and if Benny's out there that ball's going to be caught.*

I took her cherry under a cherry tree in Lakewood, New Jersey.

From this and other missions, twenty-seven of our aircraft are missing.

———————— 1964 ————————

THE DOOR TO THE BAR OPENED, AND MICHAEL CAME in, swinging his glove and spikes. He was wearing tennis shoes now. "Hi," he said, sitting down next to his father. "Can I have a coke?"

"One coke, Vinnie," Federov said. "How'd the game come out?"

"We won," Michael said.

"Anything happen in the last inning?"

"A little confusion and alarm," Michael said. He gulped at the drink Vinnie put before him. "They got two men on base and Cerrazzi was up." Michael drank again.

"What'd he do?" Federov asked.

"He walloped it. Baby, can that Cerrazzi hit that ball," Michael said. "Only this time he hit it right at Buddy Horowitz on first base, and Buddy only had to take two steps and there was the ball game. Say, Dad, do you mind if I don't ride home with you? There's a volleyball game at Andy Robert's house. You know the way home yourself, don't you, Daddy-o?"

"I know the way home all right," Federov said. "And don't be such a wise guy."

Michael laughed. He jumped from the stool. "Thanks for the coke." He started out, then stopped. "Do you mind throwing this junk into the back of the car, Dad?" He waved the spikes, tied together with their laces, looped over the back strap of the glove.

"Give them to me," Federov said.

Michael came over and put the spikes and glove on the stool next to his father. "Good old Dads," he said. "See you at dinner."

"Did you do anything in the last inning?" Federov asked. Now that he knew his son's team had won, he didn't really care about the details, but after the long, sunny afternoon, he wanted to be able to look at the young, beautiful face for thirty seconds longer.

"One grounder," Michael said carelessly, moving toward the door. "I stopped it and threw it in to second base. Nuthin'." Then a curious, experimental look came over Michael's face. "Nothing spectacular like you," he said, his voice sounding cool and suddenly mature.

"What do you mean?" Federov asked, not remembering.

"That catch," Michael said. "With one hand. And bowing." There was no doubt about the reproof in his voice.

"What was wrong with it?" Federov asked.

"You know," Michael said. "I don't have to tell you."

They were two grown men now, maneuvering, ready to attack.

"I don't know," Federov said.

"Sure you do," Michael said, standing tall in front of his father. "You were showing off. All the fellows knew it."

"Maybe I was," Federov admitted. "Is there anything wrong with it?"

"It's conspicuous," Michael said. "Unnecessary. Nobody likes his father to be conspicuous."

Federov nodded. "I see," he said. "Well, I'll see you later."

There was a last, cool look, to see how much damage had been done, and then Michael was gone.

Federov swung on his stool and stared at the bottles behind the bar. Childhood was over. The unbreakable automatic approval was over and had probably been over for years, without his having noticed it. Now the critic and competitor was present in the family, feeling for his opponent's weaknesses, testing his own powers to wound, to shape, to subjugate, to conquer, to stretch love to its breaking point.

It shouldn't have come as a surprise, Federov thought. I did it myself to my father.

He remembered how he used to hate family celebrations, when Israel would get gay on two drinks, dance whirling nimble waltzes with girls and fat cousins or, as a special crowning performance, do a Russian *khazatsky*, a difficult spectacular dance in which the dancer crouched in a sitting position, folding his arms across his chest, and kicked out his feet in an impossibly fast rhythm while everybody stood around watching, shouting and clapping time. His father would get red in the face and do it for what seemed an impossibly long time, beaming and sweating, giving himself over, for a few moments in America, to all that was young and Russian in his soul, unfettered by the drab restraints, observed but only half-understood, of a heavy-footed Anglo-Saxon society.

Benjamin had gone out of the room once while his father was dancing like that, with thirty people clapping and shouting and cheering him on. Sophie Federov had noticed the look of scorn, of disapproval, on her son's face, and had followed him out of the room. He was only eleven at the time.

"What's wrong with you?" Mrs. Federov had asked.

"Pop," Benjamin had said. "Why does he have

to be so *Jewish*? Why does he have to behave like a fool, with all those people laughing at him?"

Mrs. Federov had grabbed his wrist hard. "Get this straight," she said. "Your father is not behaving like a fool. Nobody is laughing at him. They are laughing with pleasure and admiration because your father is so happy and can dance so well and because he reminds them of some of the good things of their old life. And don't you ever say a word to him about it. And don't you grow up to be an Englishman."

Remembering, in the dark bar, Federov smiled. He wondered if Peggy would be as wise with Michael or if it would do any good. An Englishman. Were they all growing up to be Englishmen?

He finished his beer, paid, and went to the car. He tossed the spikes and glove onto the back seat and drove toward home, sniffing the faint, lifetime-familiar summer odor of leather and sweat.

Peggy still wasn't home. The gray-shingled house shook with the pound of the surf. There were too many magazines piled all over the living room. *Esquire,* January 1959. Seven *New Yorkers* from 1958, 1960, the summer of 1962. Three *National Geographics,* with their covers torn off. The *Foreign Affairs Quarterly,* a symposium on a crisis Federov barely remembered. An issue of *Encounter* from 1961. Federov picked it up. Hemingway had just killed himself and a critic spent many pages parodying and mocking Hemingway. Three issues of *Playboy*. One by one, Federov thumbed through them, opened the folded pages with the full-length glossy color photographs of plump, naked girls. How did they get girls to pose like that? Anything to get your name—or your ass—into the papers. The twentieth century. He looked at the girls. One blond, two brunettes. Waxed fruit. He collected all the magazines that had been issued before 1964 and carried them into the garage. Too damn many magazines.

He went back into the house and looked into the refrigerator to see what there was going to be for dinner. There was a pitcher of iced tea and a lot of eggs and oranges and butter and yogurt, but no meat or fowl or fish. He closed the refrigerator. He wished Peggy was home so he could tell her he didn't want to go out for dinner and to telephone for a roast of beef before the shops closed.

He went into the bedroom, vaguely thinking of lying down and taking a nap. "A nap every day will prolong your life, Ben," the doctor kept telling him. Is prolonging your life necessarily good? And until when? Fifty-one? Fifty-two? Ninety? Anyway, he couldn't take a nap. There were bills spread all over the twin beds. Peggy always did her accounts that way, spreading the bills on the beds in neat little piles. The only trouble was she would spread them all out, then leave them there and go do something else, and they would remain on the beds all day and all night until it was time to go to sleep. Then Peggy would have to gather them up and put them in a drawer and do the whole thing over again the next day. Peggy hated to do bills and the little piles of paper from Bloomingdale's and Saks and the telephone company would be spread out on the beds at least ten days a month. She was always late in paying and from time to time Federov would get a sorrowful letter from a company saying that he was in danger of being considered a bad credit risk. He didn't mind being considered a bad credit risk, but the sight of the bills spread out for years on the beds annoyed him. I *make* the money, the least she can do is spend it on time.

There was a letter on her makeup table. Federov didn't mean to look, but he saw that it was written in a man's handwriting and that it started "Dear Friend" and that it covered several pages. Because he was alone and annoyed by the bills he made a movement toward the letter. Then he stopped. He hadn't ever read any of her letters and he wasn't going to start now.

He went out of the room. Dear Friend. Hah! Somebody sneaking around his wife. Some coward. Lord Chesterfield's injunction to his stupid son— "Never write a letter to a woman you can't cool a bottle of beer on." Or was it Lord Chesterfield? Anyway, a coward.

Who knows what a woman did with her time all week down here? Like the ski resorts. The men coming up from their offices on trains every Friday night. The one from Zurich to Davos. The Cuckolds' Special. Swiss humor. Federov had never been in Switzerland, but one of his clients had told him about it. The client had had tuberculosis and had stayed more than a year in a sanitarium there. No skiing. Plenty of naps, morning *and* afternoon. Prolonging his life. He'd been cured of tuberculosis, then he'd been killed a couple of years later, driving drunk in the rain after a party in Westport.

Federov went into the living room and sat down at the piano. He couldn't play, but when he was alone like this he sometimes sat down and made up chords and tried to run them together. The chords were inevitably minor and sad, even when he was feeling fine. this afternoon they were minor and sad, too.

Where the hell was she?

How did he know she wasn't off with Dear Friend? Usually she left a note for him when she went out of the house, telling him where she'd gone and what time she'd be home. This time there was no note. Just those damn magazines.

Maybe she had just picked up and gone off with another man, and there'd be a telephone call later that night from the city or from Boston or Washington ("I'm sorry, Ben, but it just had to happen. We're very happy and we want to marry and I know you'll be reasonable about the children and you've been taking me for granted for years now.") She always said he was taking her for granted when they argued with each other. Though, really, they didn't argue too often. Not so much as most couples. Dear Friend. Absurd. She would never do anything like that.

Every married woman who had ever indicated to him that she would like to have an affair with him had started off by saying that her husband took her for granted.

Where the hell was she?

Even though he was annoyed by the clutter of magazines and nothing in the refrigerator for dinner and the crazy piles of unpaid bills on the beds, he didn't want her to be off with another man. He wanted her to be right here having a drink with him and telling him what the children had been doing all week and who was expected on Sunday and if the movie she had seen on Wednesday was ok. He wanted to be sitting there with a drink in his hand, listening to her, being a little bored, thinking maybe he'd have had more fun if he stayed in town over the weekend, but still sitting there, married, with an old-fashioned glass in his hand, not quite listening, being a little bored, and knowing the whole family was going to have dinner together at eight o'clock.

Then there was always the possibility of accidents. How many people got killed on the roads every year? Fifty, a hundred thousand? And she drove like a maniac. When he asked her why she drove that way, taking all those chances, she said it was the only way she could express herself. The one promise he could get out of her was that she wouldn't express herself while the children were in the car.

He hit a long, sorrowful, complicated chord on

the piano, a lot of flats in it, B flat, A flat, the sad notes. He saw the car over on its side, the crushed doors, the broken glass.

Where the hell was she?

1959

IT WAS IN PARIS. HE HAD BEEN INVITED TO ATTEND AN international congress on town planning. There was a chartered plane, cheap, and he'd taken two weeks off, and he and Peggy had arrived in Paris in May, just when everybody told you to arrive in Paris. But the congress had turned out to be a bore, and somehow he and Peggy weren't getting along those two weeks, and she wanted to go to just the places he didn't want to go to, and the girls in Paris made you want to die that spring, and it seemed absurd to be in that town at that season with your wife, especially since she was being sullen and unhappy most of the time.

They sat at midnight on the *terrasse* of Fouquet's, drinking whiskey, being glum with each other because the holiday had all gone wrong and the people they were thrown with had bored them and they were boring each other. Peggy was talking, but he wasn't really listening to her. He was looking at another table, where two marvelous-looking girls were sitting with an unpleasantly handsome young man of about twenty-five. The two girls and the young man had gotten out of a Facel sports car that was parked right in front of Fouquet's, and they were laughing a lot, and one of the girls was whispering into the young man's ear and making him smile, and the whole thing was intolerable to a middle-aged American sitting there, a tourist, not knowing French, with a wife he wished he'd left home.

". . . go home alone and you could stay on another week and . . ." He suddenly became conscious of what Peggy was saying.

"What's that?" he asked.

"If you could take your eyes off those girls for a second," Peggy said.

"What did you say? What's that about going home alone?"

"Well, we're not having any fun this way," Peggy said, tight-lipped, accusing. "We're just getting on each other's nerves. I can see the ice filming over your face when I say two words to you."

"God, you have an exaggerated way of talking. Ice filming. God."

"I'm sorry you don't like the way I talk," she said. "You don't have to be bothered with it. I'll take the plane home tomorrow and you can stay on here another week and enjoy yourself and get over your mood and—"

190

"Don't be a damn fool," he said, wishing he had the guts to say, "Yes, that's a good idea, I'll drive you to the airport tomorrow." "We came together," he said, "and we'll leave together."

"Well, sleep on it," she said.

"I don't have to sleep on anything," he said. "Let's get out of here."

He paid the bill and followed Peggy toward the taxi stand on the corner, self-consciously keeping himself from looking at the two girls and the unpleasantly handsome young man. The taxi was a small, rattly Simca that smelled vilely of the driver's cigarettes. They went all the way down to the Place de la Concorde and over the bridge to the Left Bank without saying a word, and they were nearly at their hotel when the car came out of the dark side street to their left, like a shell, and hit them.

Somehow, he was floating slowly over the top of the taxi, free, in midair, seeing everything clearly, having plenty of time to pull his arms and legs close to his body. He came down on his tensed forearm and rolled over on his shoulder on the pavement. There was a shock, and he knew something had happened to his knee, but there wasn't any real pain and he stood up, only staggering a little, and ran over to where the Simca was crumpled against the iron shutter of a pharmacy window. The driver was on his hands and knees on the pavement, saying *"Merde"* over and over again in a healthy voice. Peggy was down between the seats,

191

in a strange, contorted position, not moving, and there was some blood that he could see in the light from a lamppost.

Somehow, with the driver helping him, he managed to wrench a door open and drag her out. She had on a new black silk coat that she had bought the day before to show that she had been in Paris, and it was torn now and covered with blood. She groaned once as they lay her down on the pavement with the driver's sweater as a pillow. She had her hand and arm covering her face and that's where most of the blood was coming from. But she was moving and somebody said in English that it was all right, *monsieur*, the police were coming, the prefecture was just around the corner.

Groggily, kneeling beside his wife, Federov knew that it wasn't the police he needed at the moment, but whatever French he knew had deserted him and he couldn't take his eyes off Peggy lying there with her arm over her face.

"Peggy," he said, whispering as though they were already in the hospital, "are you all right?"

She made a movement of her head that could have been interpreted as a nod. Then she took her arm away from her face. There was a big cut that went from high on her forehead down her cheek. That side of her head was all matted with hair now. She put her left hand up as though it were a pad, and with her right hand made writing movements on her palm. Federov dug in his pockets for his address book and a pencil. Holding her hand steady with his, he helped her write, in the light of the lamppost. A curious small crowd of about twenty people collected around them, murmuring sympathetically.

"Can't talk," Peggy wrote. Her handwriting, surprisingly, was recognizable. "Something broken. Jaw. Are you all right?"

"Yes," he said.

"No public hospital," she wrote. "American hospital, Neuilly."

"Ok," he said.

"Call Dr. Berenson," she wrote. "Balzac 7347."

"Ok," Federov said. He had laughed at Peggy when Peggy had insisted upon telephoning her father in San Francisco for the name of a dependable English-speaking doctor in Paris. "We're only going to be there two weeks, Peggy," Federov had said, "we're not going to *die* if we have to ask the hotel to find us a doctor."

Now she not only remembered Berenson's name, but his telephone number. He, himself, couldn't even remember how to say, "Please bring me a glass of water," in French at that moment.

Peggy kept on writing. "If they have to do anything to you, remember . no penicillin. Allergy. Tell them."

"Yes." Of course, Federov had forgotten all about his allergy to penicillin.

"Call O'Connor. *Tribune*," Peggy wrote. O'-Connor was a friend of hers from school who now worked on the city desk of the Paris edition. "Ask him keep this off wires. Family not to know."

"I'll call him," Federov said.

193

Her hands dropped. She closed her eyes. For a moment it seemed to him that she was not breathing.

"Dearest," he said, bending over her.

She opened her eyes and looked up at him. She began to write again on the pad. "Cut your forehead. Hurt?"

He put his hand to his forehead. It came away sticky with blood. "Nothing," he said.

"Spoil your beauty," she wrote. "Intolerable. Love you. Never intended leaving tomorrow. Lady's trick. Love you. Where is goddam ambulance?"

When it came, it wasn't an ambulance but a small police van. There were four policemen in it who had been sitting there with submachine guns, patrolling the streets on the lookout for Algerians and OAS men who were attacking police stations and bombing the homes of political figures. The policemen put their weapons on the floor of the black van and gently laid Peggy on a canvas stretcher beside the guns. The policemen helped Federov up into the van, too. He was limping now, from his knee. The driver of the other car climbed in under his own power. He was a young man in a black shirt, who had sat on the front fender of his smashed car, aloof, smoking one cigarette after another, an aggrieved expression on his face, making up his story for the insurance people. All that seemed to be wrong with him was a cut thumb. The driver of the taxi stayed with his machine, complaining to anybody who would listen to him.

The policemen didn't want to go all the way out to Neuilly to the American Hospital, but when the van drove up to the Hôpital Necker and the young man in the black shirt got off, Federov refused to allow the policemen to touch Peggy. They grumbled, but they couldn't very well club Federov and take the injured woman out by force and they finally started toward Neuilly, with the lights on inside the van to show whatever armed Algerians were about that this was an errand of mercy and to hold their fire.

As they drove through the dark streets, surrounded by the policemen, Federov held Peggy's hand and stared down at the drawn, wounded, beloved face, pale and frightening in the bare light of the bulb attached to the ceiling of the van. If she comes out of this, Federov swore, I will never do anything to hurt her again. Never.

1964

STILL, HE THOUGHT, SITTING AT THE PIANO, HITTING B flat, she could have left a note. Damned thoughtless.

He struck a last chord. The finger that had been

cut at the baseball field when he caught the foul ball began to bleed again. Every day to its own small wound. It left a little dark red stain on the ivory of a key. He left it there and got up restlessly.

Peggy had come out of it all right, although with a bad concussion and scars and weeks of pain, but of course he had hurt her from time to time, because there is no living with anyone without hurting them occasionally. But he *had* tried to remember and keep beastliness down to a minimum. But if she walked in that minute, he knew he'd bawl her out angrily. He decided it would be better if he got out of the house. It was ominously empty and the late afternoon light made it seem lonely. It shook with the pound of the surf, a clean, polished, unstable, empty place for ghosts and heartbreak and premonition of shipwreck. He took off his shoes and socks and started out of the house to walk along the beach when the phone rang. He went back into the house and picked up the phone.

"Ben?" It was his brother's voice. "I've been trying to get you all afternoon."

"I was wandering around town. You coming out tonight?"

"No. That bitch called again," Louis said. "I've been arguing with her for hours."

"What's the matter now?" Federov asked. "I thought we had it all arranged this morning."

"Arranged!" Louis said. His voice was trembling with anger. Louis was so rarely angry that the emotion made his voice sound strange to Federov. "You can't arrange anything with that bitch for more than fifteen minutes at a time. Just long enough to call her goddam mother and listen to the goddam old lady tell her I'm taking advantage of her."

"What's she asking for now?"

"My blood, my balls, and the marrow of my bones." Louis never used language like that and Federov found that he was a little shocked by his brother's unaccustomed vulgarity. "Fifty thousand cash, the whole goddam house, *with* the pictures *and* all the books, the place in Falmouth, and twenty-five thousand a year or one-half my income, whichever is higher, plus all lawyer's fees. And the alimony to continue even if she gets married, and I know for a fact she's been screwing some fairy dress designer for two years and'll marry the sonofabitch the minute she comes back from Reno."

"Man!" Federov said.

"Man is right. Oh. I forgot. And I pay all taxes."

"You can't give her that," Federov said.

"I know it. I don't *have* that," Louis said. "I'll be peddling pencils on streetcorners."

"What're you going to do?" Federov asked.

"I'm seeing her and her goddam lawyer tomorrow. I'll try to fight out some compromise. What the hell else is there for me to do?"

"Her lawyer's going to work on Sunday?"

"That goddam Rosenthal of hers'd work on Yom Kippur, New Year's Eve and on the matinee

197

of the Second Coming of the Lord if he thought there was an extra buck in it for him," Louis said. "This is the first time in my life I'm sorry I'm Jewish and I can't call anyone a dirty-Jew shyster lawyer."

Federov couldn't help laughing. After a moment, Louis had to laugh, too. "Maybe not on New Year's Eve," he said, and he was back to the old Louis again.

"What can I do for you?" Federov asked.

"Call up Mary and tell her I'm stuck in town on business and can't come down this week."

"Why can't you call her up yourself?" Federov asked. Mary was the woman Louis intended to marry when he got his divorce. She was staying with some friends in a house down the beach for the weekend.

"I don't want to call her," Louis said. "She'll ask all sorts of questions and get all upset. Every time she knows I see the bitch she thinks somehow I won't get a divorce and we'll never get married. You know how Mary is."

"Boy," Federov said, "you sure do pick 'em."

Louis chuckled. He was not displeased about his complications with women. It was a side to his character, otherwise so tranquil, that Benamin had never been able to fathom. "Be a brother," Louis said. "Call the lady up. Tell her about the big job that came up suddenly in St. Louis or Washington or somewhere."

"She'll just call you up and find out."

"I'll turn the phone off for the weekend," Louis said.

"Okay, Brother," said Federov resignedly.

"That's a brother," Louis said. "Don't drown before Monday." He hung up.

Federov looked at the phone for a moment, sighed, then dialed the number of the house where Mary was staying. Mary answered as though she had been sitting next to the phone waiting for a call. Federov lied convincingly.

"Oh, I'm desolate," Mary said. She had a North-ampton accent, softened by Madison Avenue. She worked on television and made a great deal of money. "We had such a *fun* weekend planned. I think you ought to talk to your brother Louis," she went on. "He just works himself to the bone. Don't you agree?"

"I do, I do indeed," Federov said. "I certainly will talk to him."

He hung up and looked at the phone. How many men will *you* screw, dear? he thought. What house will *you* take? How much alimony are *you* going to ask for when your time comes, dear?

Barefooted, he went out of the house onto the dunes before the phone rang again. He made his way down to the beach and walked along the water's edge. The sea had calmed considerably, but it was still rough and menacing, with white water crashing onto the sand. The beach was deserted. He walked slowly, close enough to the water to feel the fine spray that spumed up from the waves

199

against his face. The tide-swept beach was cool and firm under his feet. His footprints, broad and high-arched, were clearly defined behind him. I am making my mark on the sands of time, he thought ironically.

He started west but stopped after a few yards when he remembered that the house in which Mary was staying was only a quarter of a mile away and overlooked the beach. If she saw him, there would be a sentimental, worrisome hour of questions and explanations, and he was in no mood for that. There is a limit, he thought, to a brother's responsibility. So he turned and went the other way, going back over his footprints.

—————————— 1944 ——————————

IT WAS IN THE ALSACE IN NOVEMBER. HIS DIVISION was out of the line, for once, and he wangled a two-day pass and a jeep and drove over the war-torn roads for a hundred and fifty miles to where Louis's A-20 squadron was based. He hadn't seen his brother for two years. He knew that as of three weeks ago his brother had been alive. He knew that because he had received a letter from his mother two days before, reporting that she had just gotten a letter from Louis.

Louis was out on a mission when Federov at last found the airfield and went into the battered stone farmhouse that served as squadron headquarters. A sergeant with thick glasses was typing at a desk. He looked up from his typing long enough to tell Federov that it was a three-group raid, target railroad yards at Essen, going in at eight thousand feet, flak usually heavy in that area, no significant fighter opposition expected, no news yet, due back at sixteen hundred hours and did he want a cup of coffee?

Federov looked at his watch. It was three o'clock. Fifteen hundred hours. An hour, minimum, to wait to find out whether his brother was alive or not that afternoon. "Thanks," he said. "Yeah."

The sergeant waved to a wrinkly aluminum pot on a primus stove under a map of northern Germany. Federov helped himself, pouring the coffee into a canteen cup on a table against the wall. He put some sugar in it from another canteen cup on the table and poured in some condensed milk from a can with holes punched in the top. The coffee was hot but awful. It was going to take years of peace, he thought, to get the taste of Army coffee out of his mouth.

"That your jeep outside?" the sergeant asked, without looking up from his work.

"Yeah," Federov said.

"Take the rotor out," the sergeant said. "This

201

squadron is composed exclusively of thieves."

Federov finished his coffee and went outside and took the rotor out and put it in the pocket of his combat jacket. He looked around him. There were tents sunk in mud and the sound of engines from the line, where ground crews were making repairs on two A-20's. An airfield. An airfield like a hundred he had seen. An airfield in bad weather, with a mean wind snapping at canvas and making men hurry to get from place to place to avoid the cold.

He went in and looked at Essen on the map. A big blob under acetate. There was an echo in his mind. Essen, Essen . . . Then he remembered. The governess on the boat to Fall River in the summer of 1935. The big, blond, smiling, bitter girl who came from Essen and who had been annoyed because he had guessed that she was a servant. He wondered if his brother had just dropped a five-hundred-pound bomb on the house in which Fräulein Gretchen Whatever had been born.

An hour is a long time when you are waiting to discover whether your brother is alive or dead. Sitting on the floor with his back against the wall in the orderly room (there was only one chair and the sergeant with glasses was sitting on it) Federov remembered taking Louis, aged nine, to the washhouse to wipe the blood off his lips after the fight Louis had just lost and to press the cold rag against the bump on Louis's forehead. And his own tears.

You knew more about your brother when you both were young than later on, before wives, separation, the watchful weighing and balancing of maturity, made you cautious about showing what you meant profoundly to each other. You could weep for a brother when you were a child.

1933

WHEN BENJAMIN WAS PLAYING FOOTBALL FOR THE small teacher's college in New Jersey that he went to, not because he particularly wanted to be a teacher, but because the tuition was free, Louis made a point of getting to see almost every game, even when it meant hitchhiking hundreds of miles to distant points in New England so that he could watch Benjamin play. During one game, when Benjamin had the wind knocked out of him and was lying senseless on the turf, Louis leaped from the stands, a small solemn boy still in knickerbockers, and ran out with the trainer to make sure that the injury was not serious. The first thing Benjamin saw when he came to was Louis's anxious, thin face peering down at him. Louis had taken off Benjamin's helmet and put it under his head and was massaging his neck as the trainer kept pushing Benjamin's legs, bending his knees methodically up to and away from the stomach to get the wind back into Benjamin's lungs.

"What the hell are you doing here?" Benjamin gasped, ashamed immediately before the squad at this grotesque breach of masculine etiquette.

"You all right?" Louis asked.

"Sure, I'm all right. Get back off the field," Benjamin said.

"You want to stay in?" the trainer asked, dumping some water from his pail over Benjamin's face.

"Come on, Ben," Louis said. "Sit out this period."

"I'm ok, I'm ok." Benjamin struggled groggily back to his feet. If Louis hadn't been there, he would have remained lying down at least another minute. Actually, he felt awful, nauseated and dizzy, and should have allowed himself to be led off the field to recover. But with Louis there, an incongruously solicitous figure with his short pants and baby face, there was no question of going back to the bench. "Get out of here," Benjamin said angrily. At the age of nineteen, he had a keen sense of what was seemly in public, and that did not include visits from his family in front of three thousand spectators in the middle of a football game.

"Ok," Louis said. "I'm going. But don't be a hero."

"Yes, Mom," Benjamin said. This was a family joke. Each Saturday before he left for a game, it was the last thing his mother said to him as he went from the house with his gear in a duffel bag over his shoulder. Later on, during the war, she said the same thing the day he left for England.

His mother and he had conducted a running argument that endured for almost eight years about his playing football. She had come to see him play only once and discovered that she could not bear to see her son battered by what she called "insane hoodlums" all afternoon. Her only comment that evening was, "Why are you always the last one to get up from the ground? I thought you were dead twenty times today. You call that a game?"

It was true that Benjamin made a practice of staying on the ground as long as possible after each play. It gave him precious minutes of added rest throughout an afternoon. He wasn't in as good shape as he should have been, mostly because he had to work at night as a sodajerk to earn the money to keep him in school, and he never got enough sleep.

His mother, who was not a lady who gave up easily, drew on friends and other members of the family to try to argue Benjamin into giving up playing football. *"Goyim nochas,* what are you proving?" was the phrase the friends and relatives used most often in describing football. The phrase meant "Gentile pleasures"—violent games, prize-fighting, mountain climbing, and wars, all things that Jews were supposed to be too intelligent to indulge in. Every time he heard it, the words infuriated Benjamin. It infuriated him because of its echo of the ghetto and what he considered the sickly assumption, incomprehensibly borrowed from their enemies, that Jews were too clever to expose themselves to danger.

"Remember," said one of his mother's friends, a high school English teacher who had been enlisted in the anti-football crusade, "remember, we are the People of the Book. We abstain from violence."

Benjamin's manners were too good to allow him to contradict an older man, and a friend of his mother's at that, so he refrained from reminding the high school teacher that the Book itself was a chaotic chronicle of murder, treachery, pillage and slaughter, and that other races, too, had been, in their way, People of the Book without noticeably eschewing violence. The Greeks, for example. The man who had written *Oedipus at Colonnus* had fought the Samians, and been a general, to boot; the *Anabasis* had been written by a man who had retreated, sword in hand, with the ten thousand; the author of *Don Quixote,* which could be considered a Book with a capital B, had been taken prisoner as a common seaman in a naval engagement; Sir Walter Raleigh, whose poetry the teacher read to the students in his English classes, had also been known to go into battle from time to time.

The human race, Benjamin would have liked to say, are the People of the Book, and the claim by one small, dispersed tribe to exclusive title was presumptuous and foolish. But all he said was, "Thanks for taking the trouble, sir. But I'm not going to stop."

"Why?" the teacher had said, annoyed. "It would give your mother so much pleasure."

"I'm not here to give my mother pleasure," Benjamin said.

"I won't repeat that to her," the teacher said.

"Thank you," Benjamin said.

And then, inevitably . . . "Benjamin, what are you *proving*?"

Benjamin didn't bother to answer.

He didn't play football to prove anything. He played because he loved it, just the way he read John Keats and played baseball and boxed in the gym because he loved it. His father, though not going on record on the subject out of respect for Benjamin's mother, quietly approved of his son's playing and enjoyed watching the games. There was some ghetto left in his father, but not that much.

During Benjamin's junior year at school, on a bitterly cold afternoon when hitting the frozen ground was like bouncing off cement, Louis was at the center of another incident. It was a rough game and the opposite team was very strong, and Benjamin was being hit harder on every play than he had been all season. He had a cold that had persisted with fever all week, and by the last quarter he was so tired he could hardly stand up. He hadn't gained more than five yards all day and had dropped a pass from his numbed hands in the open field and at his position at safety was having more and more difficulty covering the ends as they came sprinting down for long passes. The other team punted and Benjamin fumbled the kick within his own ten-yard line and the other team recovered, with a touchdown just a few feet away. The captain of Benjamin's team called a time-out to give them all a chance to recover and plot the defense against the next four plays.

In the stands, Louis was sitting behind a large boy, aged nineteen or twenty who had a hip flask from which he and his girl were nipping to ward off the cold. When Benjamin dropped the punt, the boy with the flask hooted derisively. "Hey, Federov, you bum," the boy shouted, "what're you doing in a football uniform? Why don't you try out for the girls' ping-pong team?"

The spectators on either side of the boy with the flask laughed at the gibe. Louis, in the next row, leaned over and touched the wit's shoulder lightly.

"You," he said, although the boy was at least four years older than himself and thirty pounds heavier. "Get up." Louis stood up.

The boy with the flask looked around and smiled when he saw the size of his challenger.

"What's biting you, junior?" he asked.

"You talk too much," Louis said.

"Do I?" the boy said. "What do you think you're going to do about it?"

Louis tapped him on the shoulder again, this time hard. "Come on down under the stands," he said, "and you'll see."

"You're frightening me to death, junior," the boy said.

Louis hit him with his closed fist this time, still on the shoulder.

"Ah," the boy said, still acting amused and superior, "you're a rough little feller, aren't you?" But he stood up and followed Louis down under the stands.

It was too bad that Louis missed the next two minutes after the time-out, which were the last two minutes of the game, because Benjamin redeemed himself then and there would have been no need for that brotherly trip under the stands.

The score was nothing to nothing, even though Benjamin's team had been pushed all over the field all day, and the opposing team had only two yards to go to win and four downs to do it in. Federov closed in, backing up the line, and watched the opposing quarterback. He was a small, cocky boy named Craven who had a big reputation among the minor schools that made up the schedules of both teams. He called out his signals in a sharp, barking voice, with a showy raucousness that was aimed not so much at his teammates as at the spectators in the stands.

The first play was an orthodox one—a plunge by the fullback into the center of the line. The play was piled up with no gain. The team came out of the huddle fast, and Craven began barking his signals. Somehow, with the certainty that occasionally comes to athletes at crucial moments of a game, Benjamin was sure what Craven was going to do on the play. Before the teams began to move, Benjamin slid quickly to his left. He was as confident as if Craven had said it to him in plain English that the boy was going to try to make it around right end. It had been a successful play all day for the other team and had gained a lot of ground, and Benjamin had seen enough athletes to know when a quarterback was determined to reap the glory of winning a game for himself. So even before the play started, Benjamin was there, waiting. The interference swept away his own tackle and end and the man backing up the exposed wing, but nobody had counted on Benjamin's being there, and he had a clear crack at Craven and brought him down on the line of scrimmage. Craven drove hard, but Benjamin had him dead, and there wasn't an inch gained.

Again, as the two teams lined up, Benjamin had the same serene sense of foreknowledge. He was sure that Craven, having failed once off the end, would be certain that Benjamin's team would be looking for a plunge at another point of the line. But Benjamin, tuned in relentlessly now on the sharp, shallow mind behind the flinty little street-fighter face, moved with the signals to exactly the same spot he had covered before and stopped Craven in exactly the same place.

Incredibly, Craven tried the same thing on the next play and incredibly Benjamin knew he was going to do it and was there to stop it. The final gun went off as Benjamin drove in hard and threw Craven savagely to the ground, this time for a three-yard loss. The game had been saved and Benjamin had saved it. He lay for a moment, gripping Craven's legs, feeling the hard fiber of the thigh guards under the canvas pants. For the moment he was only glad that it was all over. He got up to one knee and looked down at Craven, who was lying on his back now, breathing with difficulty because of the drive of Benjamin's last tackle. The boy's face was working with rage and disappointment, and for a second or two Benjamin thought Craven might break into tears and he felt a little wave of pity for him, all that arrogance exposed as false, all that cheap, unprofitable craftiness and vanity and glory-seeking now so openly revealed for everyone in the stadium to see.

Benjamin patted the boy's shoulder. "Tough luck," Benjamin said without cynicism.

"Fuck you, brother," Craven said bitterly. They both stood up and walked away from each other without shaking hands.

When Benjamin came out of the locker room after the game, stiff and aching and hardly able to carry his duffel bag, Louis was waiting for him in the frozen dusk. Louis's face was a mess. He had a black eye and his ear was puffed and bleeding.

"What the hell happened to you?" Benjamin asked.

"Nothing." Louis said. "I got into a little argument. Here—let me carry your bag."

"What about?"

"There was a loudmouth sitting near me and I thought he ought to be taught a lesson."

211

Benjamin examined his brother's face closely. "It looks as though you're the one who got taught the lesson," he said.

Louis touched his eye. "This—" he shrugged. "It's nothing. I busted his nose for him. The cop took him to the hospital."

"The cop?" Benjamin asked incredulously.

"Yeah. He had to come and butt in," Louis said. "He threw me out of the stadium. Anyway, there's one feller who'll be a little more careful about what he says the next time he goes to a football game."

"When did all this happen?" Benjamin asked.

"The last quarter."

"When I dropped the punt?" Benjamin said.

"Somewhere around then," said Louis. "Here, give me your bag."

Benjamin handed over the bag, and Louis swung it on his shoulder and they began to walk through the early darkness toward the bus station.

"Wait till Mom sees you," Benjamin said. "She won't let you out of her sight on Saturdays for a year."

"I can handle Mom," Louis said.

They walked in silence for a while.

"I sure was lousy out there today, wasn't I?" Benjamin said.

"You sure were," Louis said.

Then they both chuckled.

Finally it hadn't been a bad day, fever or no fever, not a bad day at all.

1944

THE SERGEANT TYPED STEADILY (RATIONS, INTELLI-gence reports, casualties, courts-martial, passes—the tapping, long war on paper, through weak eyes, blurred behind smudged thick glasses). It began to rain outside, gray, Alsatian, a permanent drip of November on soggy tents, stained uniforms, clogged rifles, scarred metal wings. The door opened, a pilot wandered in, looked around, said nothing, went out. Eternal, dangerous, dull November.

Then there was the sound of approaching engines.

"There they come," the sergeant said without looking up, without stopping his typing.

Federov heaved himself to his feet. He realized he had been dozing. In a war you slept wherever you could sit down or lie down in a warm place, even with your brother over Essen (flak usually heavy in the area, no significant fighter opposition expected).

Federov went outside, zipping the collar of his

combat jacket, putting his helmet on. There was
the thunder of engines over the field, but the
clouds, or more accurately the one, even, thick
cloud that covered the whole war that season, hid
the planes from view. Then one plane broke
through, then three, then five. Two of the planes
were firing red flares and the ambulance went
bumping across the mud to the wire landing strip
to take the wounded off.

Federov opened the door to the orderly room.
"How many planes went out from this squadron?"
he asked.

"Six," the sergeant said, never stopping his typing. "Group asked for eight, but we're all shot up.
Group yelled bloody murder."

Federov closed the door. One missing.

The planes landed bumpily, taxied. The medics
ran to the two that had fired the flares. Swiftly,
they carried out three figures, limp in fleece-lined
leather suits, two from the first plane, one from the
second.

Federov watched. One by one, the engines came
to a stop. The ambulances clanked off. A fleet of
jeeps went across the mud toward the dispersal
area. Other figures in fleece-lined leather suits, not
limp these, clambered to the ground, took off hel-
mets, climbed into the jeeps. The jeeps jolted back
toward the Operations hut fifty yards from the
farmhouse. Federov didn't move. The jeeps passed
within ten feet of him. He saw Louis sitting on the
hood of a jeep, holding onto the windshield strut.

Still, in the middle of a war, angelic, an exhausted
angel. There were five other men in the jeep.
There was no expression on Louis's face. He
looked right at Benjamin for two or three seconds,
but there was still no expression on his face. Another helmeted soldier standing around in the rain.
The jeeps stopped at the Operations hut and the
men went in to tell the G-2 what had happened;
bombs away at fourteen twenty-three hours, flak
heavier or lighter than expected, no fighter opposition or we were bounced over Mulhouse. Six bo-
gies. Two passes. They did not persist. One proba-
ble, flames seen coming out of engine. 104's. Eva-
sive action. Port engine on the *Gorgeous Irene*
seen to explode twenty-two minutes before bombing run. Smoke. Spiral down. Four parachutes
counted. On target or not on target, satisfaction, re-
proaches, alibis, where's the goddamn whiskey?

Federov walked slowly over toward the Operations hut, his boots sucking in the mud. He leaned
against the wall of the hut. The voices inside
sounded weary, emotionless, not the voices of
men.

Federov waited. The rain dripped down from
his helmet, cold on his neck and working its way
under the soggy knit collar of his combat jacket.
Another soldier standing around in the rain.

The fliers began to drift out of the Operations
hut. It was almost dark by now. Federov didn't
move. Louis passed alone three feet away from
him, walking slowly, looking down at the ground,

215

his face set in the young-old lines of the war. Federov let him get past him, two, three yards.

"Well now," Federov said.

Louis stopped. Then he turned around, very
slowly.

One of ten million men standing around in the
everlasting rain of eternal November slowly meta-
morphosed into a brother.

They embraced wordlessly.

"Lieutenant Federov," Benjamin said, "I sug-
gest one more kirsch."

"Sergeant Federov," Louis said, "you show ini-
tiative, aggressiveness, tenacity, excellent understanding of terrain, high qualities of leadership. I
am recommending you for Officer Candidate
School in the Portuguese Navy."

"*Mademoiselle! Fräulein!*" he shouted to the
old lady behind the bar. "*Deux kirschs, s'il vous
plaît. Zwei Kirschen, bitte.*"

It was midnight and they were both drunk.
They were in a smoky café in the village near the
base. They could have had whiskey in the officers'
club (a converted, leaky barn behind the squadron
headquarters, with boards leading to it so that
you wouldn't disappear in the mud when you left
it drunk after dark), but they had both wanted to
get away from the Army that night. There were
four or five old peasants in stinking leather coats
and muddy berets sitting at the other tables. There
were no young men. The young men had all been
drafted into the German Army. Years ago, in 1940,

when it meant something to be in the German Army. The old men spoke only German, and there was no expression of gratitude in their eyes as they looked at the two Americans who were the representatives of the army that had passed through the town one day and told them that they had been liberated and were now once more officially Frenchmen.

The old lady brought the kirsch bottle and poured for them both. She smelled of pigs, wet wool, small children, mud, decay.

"*Danke schön, Fräulein,*" Louis said ceremoniously. He raised his glass and considered it critically. "Best vintage of the century," he said. "Nineteen forty-four. Join the Air Force, learn languages, travel, meet the fascinating people of romantic countries, develop an exquisite palate."

They drank.

"God damn it," Louis said quietly, "when this is over and if I get out alive, I'm not going to let anything bother me again. I am just going to *breathe.*"

Two drinks later, they went out of the café. The old peasants were still there speaking German, trying to figure out ways of getting the American Army to pay for the cows that had been killed when the town had been taken two months before.

The town was blacked out and they could have been anywhere. Anywhere black. The dark side of the moon. The bottom of a well. In a whore's bedroom. In someone else's grave.

Louis took out a flashlight and they were back in Alsace again, back in November. Louis's hand was not steady and the thin beam of light wandered and it took a long time for Benjamin to get the rotor back in place. Finally he managed it and slammed the hood down. He had to hold onto the jeep to keep from falling as he made an unsuccessful effort to climb aboard.

"Sergeant Federov," Louis said, "don't you think it's dangerous to drive in your condition?"

Then they began to laugh. With forty-three missions behind them, with the miles from Cherbourg to the Rhine behind them, they laughed and laughed and laughed, clinging to each other, the light extinguished now, in the dark nowhere of November.

———————— 1964 ————————

FEDEROV WALKED IN THE DIRECTION OF THE CLUB A half-mile down the beach.

If I get out alive, I'm not going to let anything bother me again. I am just going to BREATHE.

Federov permitted himself a sigh, half-troubled,

half-ironic, remembering November, walking
barefooted on the wide deserted peaceful beach,
remembering November. His brother was breathing all right on this sunny afternoon in September, 1964, but anybody who could shout over
the telephone, "My blood, my balls, and the marrow of my bones," could hardly pretend he wasn't
being bothered by anything.

Wars do not teach as much as one would like to
believe. The guns fall quiet but the soul still
trembles.

Federov could see the wide veranda of the Club
now. It was deserted, except for two small figures,
shapeless bundles of sweaters, skirts, scarves, under
a striped parasol.

Federov had never been inside the Club and had
never swum off its beach, although the beach,
from the high tide line seaward, was public. The
Club, except for two or three tame token speci-
mens who were extraordinarily rich or extraordinarily well connected, wasn't for Jews.

*Israel, Israel, my name is Israel and I want you
to get that man out of my house.*

And, *Tell them I'm not a Jew*—the voice of his
Uncle George, the hoarse, workingman's voice—
I'm an American. I was born in Cincinnati.

Cincinnati! Don't make me laugh. All they'll remember is Jew.

      For the walls that are overthrown ...
      We sit in solitude and mourn.

For our majesty that has departed ...
We sit in solitude and mourn.
For our great men who lie dead ...
We sit in solitude and mourn.

1957

IT WAS AT THE FUNERAL OF HIS FATHER THAT HE SAW his Uncle George for the first time since the evening when George, with his bandaged head, had come to the house in Harrison to ask for a loan. Death binds families, transiently and too late.

Now nearly sixty, George had grown into a scholarly looking man, thinned, bowed, the violence fined out of his face by suffering, by a late-flowering interest in books, by a self-discipline in training a brute intelligence that had always been there dormant and caged. Even his voice had become lighter, with an educated and polite tone to it, and his eyes, still a clear deep blue, now looked out on the world forgivingly and with humor. He had stopped working with his hands and for some years had been, not surprisingly, a minor official in the National Maritime Union.

Benjamin felt himself attracted to the man he had not seen since the silent, adolescent farewell at the foot of the stairs in Harrison, New Jersey. He went over to George, standing in a corner of the dining room, where the family were gathereed around the cold meats and the whiskey bottles after the cemetery.

The two men shook hands and George said, examining Benjamin, "Well, you turned out better than I thought. You're not even fat. How old are you now?"

"Forty-three," Benjamin said.

"Thirty years . . ." The old man shook his head. "Some day you must make me a full report."

They talked briefly of Israel Federov. "Did you ever hear him say he forgave me?" George said.

"No," Benjamin said.

George nodded. "I'm sorry," he said. "Your father was a good man, but he was confused about the nature of patriotism. He thought it was abasement before authority. It's a first-generation Jewish disease."

"Not necessarily," Benjamin said, although he didn't feel he had to defend his father. "What about the hundredth-generation Germans who felt the same thing?"

George smiled. "You're right. I hadn't thought about it. As I get older, I guess I see everything more and more from the viewpoint of a Jew. *That's* the real disease."

Federov saw George off and on after that, taking

his uncle to dinner in a steak place that George liked near Pennsylvania Station. Sometimes George showed up with a man he thought might interest his nephew, sometimes alone. One evening he came into the restaurant with a tall, slender man younger than he, but with white hair. "Sam Sternberger," he said, introducing him to Federov. "He's one of the lawyers who tries to keep us all out of jail when we do naughty things like asking for showers in the foc's'le."

They ordered drinks and oysters and steaks and while they were eating, Sternberger entertained Federov with courtroom anecdotes and instances of corruption on the part of shipowners and government officials.

"Hey," George said, interrupting Sternberger in the middle of a description of how he had had to deal with a judge on the take for a bribe. "Hey, Sam, tell him about you and the Sacco-Vanzetti case. I didn't see this boy"—he waved a fork at Federov—"for thirty years because his father kicked me out of the house because I was in the demonstration in Boston that day. How old were you then, Benny?"

"Thirteen," Federov said.

"I had a lump on the side of my head as big as a cantaloupe," George said. "A cop got me against a wall and really laid it on. He must've weighed two hundred pounds. Tell him, Sam."

"I was a student at the time," Sternberger said. "Columbia. My family lived in New York. I was majoring in philosophy. Don't ask me why. I had a job that summer selling frozen custard on the boardwalk in Coney Island. All of a sudden I got a telephone call from my mother. I had to come right home, she said. She wouldn't tell me why—" He speared a slice of tomato from a platter and put it on his plate next to his steak and French-fried potatoes. "Nobody ever said no to my mother. Not in a German-Jewish family. So I took off my apron and told the boss I didn't know when I was coming back and I took the subway up to Morningside Heights, where we lived. My mother was waiting for me in the kitchen. She was finishing wrapping some sandwiches for me. She had a bag packed for me and a ticket on the train for a round trip to Montreal, Canada. 'Go,' she said, 'go to Montreal. Your Tante Elsa needs you. She is dying. And she needs you tomorrow.' 'Yes, Mama,' I said. You took orders in my family. 'But why tomorrow?'

"'Dummkopf,' my mother said, 'don't you ever read the newspapers?'

"'Yes, Mama, I read the newspapers,' I said. It wasn't true. I thought that a man who was studying Kant and Hegel and Plato insulted his intelligence by reading newspapers, but I couldn't explain this to my mother. You couldn't explain anything to my mother. 'But why does Tante Elsa need me tomorrow?' I asked her."

Sternberger had the lawyer's gift, which Federov had always admired, of being able to talk in coherent, unhesitating, grammatical sentences. Even in the minute or two that Sternberger had been telling the story, the image of the austere mother in the kitchen and her imperious domination of the young, unformed philosophy student who had just put off the white apron in Coney Island was clear and real.

" 'The Italians,' my mother said, 'the two anarchists—they are executing them tomorrow. You know your Tante Elsa, you know how she feels about this. And she is dying, besides. It is one day she cannot be alone.' "

"His aunt was famous," George said. He told Federov the name. It was the name of a woman who hadn't been forgotten even after all these years, a professed anarchist, a woman who had gone to Russia during the Revolution, who had sat with Lenin on platforms, who had broken with the Bolsheviks, who had been implicated but never convicted in the attempted assassination of a great industrialist in the Middle West. She hadn't been convicted, but she had been deported, at the time of the Palmer raids, in the 1920's, first to Mexico and from Mexico to Canada.

"My mother hadn't spoken to her sister Elsa for years," Sternberger went on, comfortably chewing on his steak. "When my aunt came back from Russia my mother told her she'd disgraced the family name and that she was ashamed to show her face on the street and in the synagogue and that she never wanted to see her again. She never did, either. But it was a big family, my mother had four brothers, and they kept in touch with Tante Elsa and my mother got all the news. And I myself went to visit her every Christmas.

" 'She has tuberculosis,' my mother said. 'The doctors only give her days to live, she can't be alone tomorrow. And you're the only one in the family she likes. You're the only one in the family she says isn't German. I suppose she means that as a compliment,' my mother said. 'Maybe she's right. Who knows what goes through that poor woman's head? Anyway, you're the only one she ever asks about in her letters to the rest of the *Mespucheh.*' "

" '*Mespucheh*' means 'family,' Benny," George said.

"That much Yiddish I know," Federov said.

"Just in case. You never can tell with you young fellers."

Sternberger went on. " 'She says you're wasting your time studying those old dead Greeks, Elsa,' my mother said. 'She has an opinion on everything, that woman. But no matter. You go to Montreal. You stay by her side. You represent the family. You give her comfort. Here'—my mother gave me the sandwiches. 'Put these in your pocket. Eat. The tickets cost enough as it is, there's no sense in making the thieves in those dining cars rich. And God knows what they feed you, with all those fancy prices.' "

Sternberger smiled faintly, enjoying the memory of that powerful, obstinate woman, his mother, that strong voice silenced these many years, that rigid code of honor, that pride of family, that queenlike insistence on traditional deportment, now only a subject for amusing anecdotes at weddings and funerals.

"So I went to Montreal," Sternberger continued. "I sat up all night. Aside from being thrifty, my mother thought Pullman cars were immoral. All those people, men and women all mixed up, sleeping together with only wavy little curtains between them. Men sleeping on top of women, women sleeping on top of strange men.

"My aunt was living in one room in a boardinghouse. A dying neighborhood. Big old mansions in what used to be a rich quarter of the city, now cut up into small apartments, boardinghouses. Spinsters, widows, old bachelors, people with small pensions, people with night jobs, a hot plate for cooking behind a screen in the corner of the room, everything on the decline and no hope of its ever getting better. My aunt's room was tiny, filled with books and papers. Cigarette butts overflowing from saucers and a coffee pot always going. Somehow, wherever my aunt lived, even though she was German and had lived in North America most of her life, her rooms looked as though they were in a poor quarter of Moscow under the Czar. No windows open, even in summer, because she was dying. 'I have the winter of the grave in my bones, Sam,' she told me that morning, all wrapped up in sweaters. Everything she wore was brown or black or dusty green. Everything about her, her clothes, her complexion, her hair, was the color of dust. She was nearly a skeleton already. Her face was sharp, translucent, like the edge of a seashell. She kept walking up and down that little room all morning, smoking one cigarette after another, holding the cigarettes the Russian way, with the hand cupped under them, so weak she had to hold onto the back of a chair, onto the bedpost, the edge of the washbasin, my shoulder, to keep from falling. But she wouldn't sit down. 'I am like an old horse,' she said. 'If I sit down, I will never get up again.'

" 'Your mother is a narrow, ignorant woman,' my aunt said. 'If she were a man she would be a tax collector in Prussia. Her horizon is the kitchen stove. She has only slept with one man in her whole life. Your father. Imagine the outlook on life of a woman who has only made love to one man. Made love! Hah! Taken off her corset for ten minutes on a Saturday night twice a month. She thinks I'm crazy. A woman rules the house, she thinks, men change the world. But she sent you here to me today. For that I forgive her everything, tell her. For today. Somewhere inside the corset there is the remnant of a heart, she remembers that we slept in the same bed together when we were children, that we gathered raspberries in the fields along the Rhine in the summer in white dresses and blue aprons, that we stood beside the grave of our grandfather in the cemetery in Cologne when we were both under ten years old. I thank her for it, tell her, she sent me her son when I needed him.'

"She kept tottering from chair to bed to basin," Sternberger said, "and I was afraid she was going

to fall and die right then and there. She couldn't
stop talking and she couldn't stop smoking and she
couldn't stop walking up and down. And it wasn't
because she was dying. She had a contempt of
death. She wouldn't cry for anybody else's and she
wouldn't cry for her own. She wouldn't cry for Sacco and Vanzetti, either. 'What a farce,' she said.
'Those hypocritical holy Puritans from Boston pretending they are saving the world, pretending they
are upholding justice, proud of themselves because
they are killing two poor little Italian workmen.
Beware people in power, Sam, beware the rich.
They're frightened somehow their money is going
to be taken away from them, they strike out blindly—in all directions, at people passing by in the
streets, at children, at poets, at shadows, at two little Italians. Beware systems. Beware rulers. They
are all the same. Everything to keep them where
they are—on the workingman's back. And don't
think the Russians are better. They're worse. The
hypocrisy is deeper. They tell the world they are
workingmen, they are for the workingman. Liars.
Rockefellers in caps. Bismarcks without a tie. All
for effect. How many Vanzettis they've killed already, how many poor dumb Saccos. They could
sit down at lunch with the Governor of Massachusetts, they could shake hands with Judge Webster
Thayer, and if you changed their clothes nobody
could tell the difference.' "

Sternberger finished his beer, put the glass down
on the tablecloth. He had long, fine hands and he
used them with precision. He paused. He was re-

mote. He was not in a crowded and noisy restaurant in New York any more. His hair was not white. He was a young philosophy student again in a dingy room in Montreal, awed by the elemental cry of outrage of a dying woman, a woman through whose veins ran the same blood as his but who, as if with a contemptuous actor's aside on a stage, had cut her ties with family, with security, with everything small and safe, to plunge into bitter depths where only courage counted, where only the purest and most dangerous honesty could be tolerated, where love was nothing, sympathy nothing, hope nothing, conviction everything . . .

It's amazing, Federov thought, how everybody remembers every detail of that one day in 1927. Like the survivors of Pompeii who watched from afar as Vesuvius stained the sky and who must have described with grieving accuracy the flaming rock, the day-long cloud, each moment of the death of the city, to their great-grandchildren; like the four or five inhabitants the Germans had neglected to kill when they wiped out Ourador and who would always know what the church looked like as it burned, what the cries sounded like from within.

A waiter came over and put three glasses of beer on the table. The movement, so close to Sternberger, brought him back to today, to the restaurant, to the men at the table with him. He took a long draught of the beer, then played with the glass, tapping lightly at its stem.

"She kept coughing and coughing into handkerchiefs," Sternberger went on. "She had a dozen handkerchiefs on her, in pockets, tucked into her sleeves, into the sash around her bathrobe, everywhere, and she would cough so hard I thought the final hemorrhage had to start any minute.

" 'And me, me, your beloved Aunt Elsa,' she said after the worst fit of coughing. 'Here it is noon, August twenty-third, 1927, the two men are walking to the electric chair, the whole world is holding its breath in horror, and your aunt, who has been tortured by the police of four countries, who fought in revolutions, who has addressed meetings of fifty thousand people, whose name is hated by every hypocrite in the world, where is your aunt? In Boston, screaming in agony, denouncing this crime? Waiting with a gun to kill the *real* criminals? No. In a little room in Canada, a hopeless country with no history, no future, a continent of bigots, coughing my lungs out, dying for no purpose. And where should I be? In Charlestown Prison. Myself. Walking to the electric chair. Being the martyr to wake up a billion people from their sleep. The whole world is looking at this one execution. It is *our* crucifixion. At this moment they are making two saints for the next two thousand years. And who are these saints? Two poor, obscure, illiterate men, who don't even know what's happening to them. They are victims, not martyrs. THEY DO NOT KNOW THEIR GLORY and so they do not deserve it, they are robbing me of it, me, me, me . . .' "

Sternberger had stopped eating, as had Federov and George, as the smooth, easy lawyer's voice dominated the hum of the busy restaurant, the voice low, but burning with the passion that had not diminished in thirty years, the voice that remembered the last terrible phrase of his aunt's life: THEY DO NOT KNOW THEIR GLORY.

Sternberger shook his head, returning from the past. "She died four days later," he said. "All alone. I was back at Coney Island selling frozen custard on the boardwalk. When I got home from Montreal my mother didn't ask me a single question about what had happened there. All she said was, 'One of your hoodlum friends is here, he came last night, he said he had no place to sleep.' It was a classmate of mine from Columbia. They'd kicked him out of the YMCA on Twenty-third Street because he'd thrown a chair out the window and broken a skylight at noon, the only way he could think of at the time to protest the execution." Sternberger was quiet for a moment.

"After my mother died in 1940, we finally got my aunt's coffin down from the cemetery in Montreal and buried her next to her sister in Queens. I didn't tell anybody about my aunt for years. I was ashamed of her." He smiled a little sadly. "I don't really know what to think about her even now," he said. "I go out to Queens once a year and put some flowers on the two graves." He looked at his watch. "I'm sorry," he said, getting up. "I'm late. I have to go home."

The next night Federov went to a party at the Staffords'. It was a big party in their house on East

Seventy-eighth Street and there was the usual hap-hazard mixture of generations and professions that John Stafford gathered around him—actors, politicians, boys from Yale, young married couples who worked for magazines and publishing houses, people who were there because they were hand-some or poor or seldom invited anywhere else.

Sternberger's story about his aunt had haunted Federov all day long and, even though Stafford was surrounded by a group of young people who were standing with him at the bar, Federov began to tell Stafford about the old lady in Boston and her saints for the next two thousand years. When he mentioned the names of Sacco and Vanzetti, he saw blank looks on the faces of the youngsters.

Stafford laughed as Federov stopped in midsen-tence. "They never heard of them, Ben," he said. "They don't give that course in good schools."

"I don't believe it," Federov said.

"They came in late," Stafford said. "They were born after 1920."

"Even so . . . ," Federov said.

"Ask them."

"My dear young lady," Federov said to a blond girl in a red dress, "can you tell me who Sacco and Vanzetti were?"

"Well . . ." The girl was embarrassed.

"How about you?" Federov turned to her escort, who seemed about twenty-three. "Do you know about them?"

"Vaguely," the boy said. "To be honest—no."

"They were anarchists back in the early twenties," Federov said, fighting back what he knew as an irrational anger, "a shoemaker and a fish peddler in Massachusetts, and they were convicted of murdering a man in a holdup. But the general feeling was that they were innocent and they were convicted not because they had had anything to do with the crime, but because of their political opinions. Though Oliver Wendell Holmes—" Again he saw the look of puzzlement on the young faces. He laughed, his anger gone. "He was a Justice of the Supreme Court," Federov explained. "Anyway, what I wanted to say was that despite all the outcry, Holmes thought the men were guilty and he wrote somewhere that the case was being turned into a text by the Reds. But whether he was right or wrong, at the time many people who were not Reds thought the case would never be forgotten and I guess I thought the same thing and that's why I'm surprised when anybody doesn't know all about them."

"I heard of them," said a young girl at the far end of the bar. She was pretty, not American. Feerov had met her and her husband several times. She was Belgian, but had married an American after the war. She was more than thirty years old, but she looked younger.

"How did you hear of them?" Federov asked.

"From my father and mother," the girl said. "In Belgium."

"What were they—your father and mother? Socialists?"

The girl laughed. "Nobility," she said. There

was a trace of mockery in her voice. "They used to play croquet on the lawn after dinner when I was a little girl. You know how you put your foot on your own ball and tap it to send your opponent's ball off the course?"

"Yes," Federov said, curious now.

"They called that the Sacco-Vanzetti shot," the girl said. "You hit Sacco—I guess the noise the mallet made against the ball sounded something like 'sacco' or 'socko'—and you knocked Vanzetti off the course. It was a family joke . . ." There was silence in the room.

The girl looked around, embarrassed. "I'm sorry," she said, although what she was sorry about would have been difficult for her to explain and for the others to understand. "I suppose . . . in Belgium, at the time, it must have seemed—well—remote . . ."

1964

FEDEROV HAD REACHED THE BEACH IN FRONT OF THE Club by now. Two old ladies under the parasol stared coldly at him. A hundred times a summer they complained about the law, demagogically inspired, which permitted outsiders to spoil their view of the ocean merely by keeping below the high-tide line on the beach. Lonely sentries, old bones wrapped in scarves, windswept and discarded, unpleasant at a distance, unpleasant close up, menopaused, everlastingly dissatisfied, under a striped parasol on a bare white beach, they guarded the gates of the past.

The sea was still running strong, but now Federov, who had been walking with his head down watching his toes squash into the damp sand, saw that there were four boys, aged about seventeen, out in the rough water, being tossed about on rubber mattresses on which they were trying to ride the waves. They were not in any immediate trouble, but Federov knew the coast well and how treacherous rip tides could build up in this kind of swell and pull the strongest swimmer out to sea. He tried to shout to the boys to come in, feeling the disapproval of the old ladies behind his back at this unseemly noise. But the crash of waves drowned his voice and the boys either did not see him gesturing or purposely ignored him.

There was a catamaran on blocks high on the beach, but without oars. It was late in the afternoon, the red flag had been up all day and the two lifeguards who were usually on duty were not to be seen.

One of the boys was overturned by a wave and it was only by luck that another boy grabbed his mattress as it went by and held onto it.

"Fools," Federov said aloud.

DEATH BY WATER.

The lake was down the hill, eight hundred yards away, out of sight of the camp. The camp was in the Adirondacks. It was a coed camp, the girls' bunks separated by a thick grove of pines from the boys' side. Benjamin was to get seventy-five dollars for working as a counselor for nine boys between the ages of eight and ten for the summer. The camp was owned by a Mr. Kahn, a small, roostery nuisance of a man with ulcers and a bad temper, who could be heard screaming at the cooks in the kitchen that they were wasting food. He also complained constantly to the counselors that they were losing too many baseballs and not being careful enough in checking the campers' laundry each week and that he alone, poor, sorely beset, pitiful Morris Kahn, out of his own pocket, would have to pay the parents for all the missing shirts and sweaters at the end of the season.

The camp was badly run. There wasn't even a doctor, just a slovenly nurse who was trying to chalk up the all-time camp record for sleeping with the most counselors in the summer. Campers and counselors alike were permitted to go down to the lake whenever they liked and swim without supervision. After taps, counselors from the boys' side could be seen walking openly, carrying blankets, to rendezvous with the girl counselors in secluded glades, wet with the cold dew of the mountain nights. The tennis courts were bumpy, the baseball field unkempt, the kitchen dirty; the atmosphere was slack, the counselors neglected their charges and spent their time scheming how they could get extra free time and making deals with each other to exchange their weekly twenty-four hours off so that they could amass three days of liberty in a row and flee from Mr. Kahn. If Benjamin, who had an exaggerated sense of order and responsibility, hadn't needed the seventy-five dollars so badly he would have quit the first week.

The counselor in the bunk next to Benjamin's was a man called Schwartz, a physical-training teacher in a high school in New York. He was a well-muscled, wiry, short man with a dark complexion, made even darker by the sun so that he looked like an Arab. He was a stupid man, but he was more conscientious than the others and he and Benjamin became friendly on the basis of their common disgust with the way the camp was run. Schwartz was older than the other counselors, nearly thirty, and he was engaged to be married in October. He showed the photograph of his fiancée to everybody again and again. It was the photograph of a dumpy little woman with dyed blond hair and thick legs. "Isn't she beautiful?" Schwartz asked eagerly each time he brought the snapshot out of his foot locker.

Schwartz's fiancée came to visit him from New York every two weeks, and Mr. Kahn, for reasons best known to himself, let Schwartz off on those Friday and Saturday nights to sleep with the beauty in a small hotel nearby.

"Yes," everybody agreed, "she's beautiful." Often when Schwartz showed the woman's photograph, he left his foot locker open. There was a box of about thirty condoms, neatly and prominently arrayed on the top shelf of the foot locker. Schwartz smiled widely when people noticed the condoms. He was a simple man and proud to prove that he, an ordinary high school teacher, had a mistress, and one of such extreme beauty.

In the middle of August, the night before the lady was due to arrive, two of the counselors stole into Schwartz's bunk, opened the foot locker and with a needle carefully made little invisible holes in every one of the condoms and then put them back in their box, arranged just as Schwartz had left them. The practical jokers told most of the others counselors what they had done, but not Benjamin, because they knew Benjamin was a friend of Schwartz's.

Condoms were a standard source of humor, and one of the counselors who had pierced the holes in Schwartz's collection added to his reputation as the camp wit by saying, "There's going to be a little

Schwartz in this camp a lot sooner than anyone realizes."

Schwartz was a physical-culture fanatic. He did a hundred push-ups a day and ran a mile each evening before dinner. But with all that, he had never learned really to swim. Even so, each morning after reveille, rain or shine, he would rush down to the lake with the swimming instructor, a man called Olson, and dive in, staying close to the dock, ignoring the coldness of the lake at that hour and brushing his teeth in the water. He had the theory that this exercise was good for his gums.

Olson was a huge, muscular man who played water polo for a Midwestern school. He was taciturn, sleepy-eyed and in love with his own body. All day long, except when he was swimming, he could be seen stroking his chest and his ridged belly slowly with caressing, self-admiring hands. He talked little and did his job badly and spent a good part of his time just lying in bed, outside the reach of discipline. He rarely talked and nobody knew him very well, not even the fifteen-year-old girl who sneaked out of her bunk every night to meet him in the forest. Aside from swimming a couple of miles a day to get ready for the water-polo season, he was completely uninterested in everything and everybody connected with the camp.

On the morning of the Friday that Schwartz's fiancée was due to arrive, Schwartz and Olson went down as usual to the lake after reveille. It was a raw, drizzly day and they were alone. They dove in, Schwartz staying close to the docks, Olson swimming sixty yards out with one breath, then surfacing, taking another breath, and swimming back without taking his head out of the water. All this came out later.

Olson swam to the dock, climbed out, gave Schwartz his toothbrush, with the ribbon of paste neatly on it, and went to the shore end of the dock to dry himself off and put on his bathrobe and moccassins. They swam naked in the mornings. When Olson turned around again, Schwartz was gone. Olson looked over the edge of the dock. The water was black and chopped by the wind. Olson saw nothing. Then he ran up the eight-hundred-yard hill to the camp to get help.

Schwartz had been under the water more than ten minutes when they finally found him and brought him to the surface. He was dead but nobody on the dock wanted to admit it. Olson and Benjamin took turns at artificial respiration, working on Schwartz, who had been stretched on his stomach, with one arm folded under his head. Olson and Benjamin spelled each other, kneeling over the still body, pressing down with both hands on Schwartz's back, then slowly releasing the pressure in a rhythm that they hoped would restore normal breathing. Kahn had come running down in his bathrobe, a ruffled, uncombed, screechy, barnyard bird of a man, shouting at everybody, saying, "Oh, my God," and "The idiot," and "This is the end," and peering again and again into Schwartz's calm open dead eyes and saying, "There's life there. I

know it. I know it." He made sure immediately
that no one besides Olson and Benjamin and the
two other counselors who had run down with Olson could approach the lake, and he hurried up
the hill himself to call the hospital in the nearest
town to send an ambulance and a pulmotor and to
tell all counselors that the routine of the camp was
to go on as usual that morning, except that all
swimming was canceled because of the bad
weather.

On the dock, Benjamin was working over
Schwartz. Olson had a towel wrapped around his
head and neck, and pulled his bathrobe tighter
around him to avoid catching cold.

The other two counselors by now had been
posted out of sight as guards to block the way to
the lake.

"He's croaked," Olson said flatly, making sure
he was dry all over. "We're working on a stiff. It's a
waste of time."

Benjamin didn't say anything. He worked on
the cool brown body of his friend, push, release,
count, push, release, count. He knew Schwartz was
dead, but he didn't say anything, either about that
or about Olson's running up the hill for help,
knowing that nobody could get back down to the
lake in less than ten minutes, instead of diving in
immediately and hunting for Schwartz while there
was still a chance of saving him. The water off the
dock was only twenty feet deep and Olson could
stay under for three minutes at a time when necessary. He had run up the hill for one of three rea-

sons—panic or stupidity or cowardice. Benjamin never decided which.

A half-hour later, Kahn came back, standing on the running board of the ambulance. He had waited outside the gate of the camp so that he could cut the ambulance off and bring it down a side road, where the campers, now at their breakfast in the mess hall, could not see it and start rumors flying. The young doctor in the ambulance turned Schwartz over, put the rubber mask on Schwartz's face and started the machine going. By the expression on the doctor's face, Benjamin knew that the doctor knew he was wasting his time. Nobody said anything. Olson and Benjamin and Kahn stood off to one side in the fine drizzle, watching the doctor and the ambulance driver work the machine, the only sound the chop of the water against the pilings of the dock and the desolate, hoarse, almost animal sigh of the pulmotor and the nervous gasping of Mr. Kahn as he smoked cigarette after cigarette and tried to will poor Schwartz to start earning his salary again and breathe.

Occasionally, almost negligently, the doctor knelt and put his hand on Schwartz's wrist to feel for a pulse that was never going to be there again, or strip back the blanket that now covered the body and listen with his stethoscope for the beating of a heart that wasn't going to beat again. The doctor would listen patiently for a minute, then remove the stethoscope from his ears and let it dangle around his neck and pull the blanket into place and stand up.

Each time, Kahn would ask excitedly, "Well?" The doctor would shake his head. He looked bored. The pulmotor made its hoarse, agonized sigh in the drizzle. Schwartz lay still. His eyes closed now about the rubber mask, he looked merely asleep. Only his complexion was changing. Under the Arab brown of his skin there was an indigo tinge. It was the first time Benjamin had ever seen a dead man.

It was misty and the forest on the other side of the lake was lost in the enveloping grayness. They could have been on the banks of a limitless ocean. Whales could have been cruising offshore, battleships could have been making their way through the mist to foreign ports.

After an hour, the doctor said, "Well, that's that."

The ambulance driver stopped the pulmotor. The sudden silence was a relief. Olson and Benjamin carried the body, still wrapped in the blanket, to the ambulance and put it in the back. Kahn insisted on going to the hospital in the ambulance. "Listen, boys," he said to Benjamin and Olson, his tone wheedling, pleading, "don't say anything up there." He gestured in the direction of the camp. "Nothing much happened, eh, boys? Schwartz is ok, ok, heh? A little heart attack, maybe, heh? The cold water. He's alive, see, we're taking the best of care of him. No expense is being spared. He has a private room in the hospital, so he can rest, heh, no visitors for the time being, naturally, heh? And don't tell even *that* to the children. To the other

243

counselors, if necessary. If the rumor gets around that he drowned, there won't be a boy or a girl left here by tomorrow morning. I'll be ruined. He'll be all right, won't he, Doc?"

"No," the doctor said.

"What do you know?" Kahn shouted. "A young inexperienced boy like you, just out of school. We'll get a specialist, a heart man, the best."

"Ok, mister," the doctor said, bored. He got into the back of the ambulance with the corpse.

Kahn climbed up beside the driver. He made the driver go down a rough road all around the other side of the lake, even though it took thirty minutes longer to the hospital that way, because, he said, he didn't want to take the chance of disturbing the children in the camp unnecessarily and spoiling their holiday.

Olson and Benjamin watched the ambulance drive away, disappear into the drizzle, jolting on the rough dirt road.

"Well," Olson said, "I'm going to get me some breakfast."

He and Benjamin climbed the hill together. They didn't speak. When they got to the mess hall, the boys had finished eating, but there were whispering groups of counselors who rushed over to Olson and Benjamin and bombarded them with questions. Benjamin refused to say anything.

"He had a heart attack," Olson told the other counselors as he drank his delayed coffee and munched on his scrambled eggs and rolls. "He's resting in the hospital. The water was awfully cold this morning."

That night, Olson went out with his blanket to meet his fifteen-year-old girl as usual.

Nobody remembered about Schwartz's fiancée, and, when she arrived at the camp at five o'clock in the afternoon, it was Benjamin who had to tell her that Schwartz was dead. By then, Kahn had come back to the camp, his face sober, but his voice guardedly triumphant, with the news that the specialist had agreed with the diagnosis. Schwartz had died from a heart attack; he had not drowned.

Not a single camper was taken home before the end of the season by his or her parents. A new rule was put into effect. There was to be no swimming except at specified hours with every counselor on duty on the dock and on the raft and in boats around the swimming area.

Benjamin didn't speak to Olson again all the rest of the summer. Olson didn't seem to mind or even notice.

Schwartz had no family that anybody knew of, and his foot locker, the condoms tactfully removed, was sent back to Schwartz's fiancée in the city. She did not become pregnant that year.

THE WAVES POUNDED ON THE BEACH, RAINBOWS IN the spume, lit by the setting sun. The four boys were still out there in the rough sea. Federov didn't know whether it was because they wanted to stay out or because they couldn't get in. Either way, and whether they knew it or not, they were in danger. They still paid no attention to Federov's shouts, which were lost in the pound of the surf.

Death by water.

Federov looked up at the verandah. A waiter in a white coat was serving the old ladies tea and muffins. Federov went up toward the verandah and stopped in front of the old ladies.

"Good evening," he said.

The old ladies looked up from their tea. They nodded tightly. Guillotine mouths, munching on marmalade. The acid lines of disappointment and privilege pulled the thin lips down like barbed wire. The mottled hands tinkled the china cups.

"Those boys out there"—Federov gestured toward the ocean—"they shouldn't be out in this kind of sea. I wonder if you could ask the waiter to see if he can find one of the lifeguards and have him go out in the catamaran and round them up. I'll go out with him, tell him, if he thinks I can help."

The two old ladies looked out at the boys fighting the waves.

"It doesn't look so bad to me," one of the old ladies said. She had a voice like thin glass. "I've seen people swim in much worse off this beach. Haven't you, Catherine?"

The second old lady surveyed the Atlantic Ocean professionally. "Much worse," she said.

"Still—" Federov began.

"I don't like to interfere in the pleasures of strangers," the first old lady said. She spoke with full appreciation of her own good manners.

"They're not strangers," Federov argued, feeling foolish. "I'm sure they're from around here. In fact, I think I recognize—"

"Edward," the first old lady said to the waiter, "are those boys members?"

"No, ma'am," Edward said. "They're from the town."

He was a Negro and Federov had a fleeting notion that Edward didn't care who drowned and who didn't drown as long as he was white.

Another acid dropping of two mouths, twin guillotines. "I'm sorry, sir," said the old lady who had spoken before. "You heard the waiter. They are not members."

Federov laughed. He was surprised at the noise as it came from his throat. The two mouths went down, blades.

He turned and saw he hadn't needed to bother. The boys had caught a big wave and the four mattresses came swirling in, sweeping their riders high up onto dry sand. The boys jumped up, laughing.

Federov strode down to them. "Ok," he said. He knew one of the boys, Jimmy Redford, the son of the owner of the stationery store the Federovs patronized. "Ok, Jimmy, if I ever see you do anything as foolish as that again, I'll grab you and take you to your father, and if he doesn't beat the stuffing out of you, I will. That's a promise, Jimmy. Did you hear me?"

"Yes, sir." The boys stood in a short, guilty row, looking as if they had been caught by a policeman as they were breaking windows or lined up in juvenile court for buying beer illegally.

Federov started back toward home as the boys dried themselves and put pants on over their wet trunks. The sun was low in the west as he walked into it.

The afternoon whirled in his head.

They are not members. Sacco and Vanzetti, guilty or innocent, were not members. He and his father, the old catcher, and his brother (flak heavy in the area) and his wife and son (Old Pope Sinister the First) and his eleven-year-old daughter were not members. Pat Forrester, her new party dress hanging uselessly in the closet, her ears

248

stuffed with cotton against the celebrating bells, was not a member. Sternberger's aunt, coughing her lungs up in Montreal (THEY DO NOT KNOW THEIR GLORY), was not a member. His Uncle George (I should have cried my tears, too, for the two Italians), clubbed by a Boston cop, was not a member. John Stafford with character-istic tact, had quietly resigned and was no longer a member. John Fitzgerald Kennedy, although ac-cepted by the committee on the day of his birth, had declined the invitation and was not a member. You heard what the waiter said.

Now list the members. Bryant, laughing, trying to remember the song *Sacco, Vanzetti, What did you do?*, was a member. Cohn, that all-'round boy, gifted, heartless, dead, was a member. Article 7: *It is understood that there is nothing in the club rules that guarantees that members are immune to suffering or death.* The club was no fly-by-night or-ganization it had its history; according to Henry IV the Duc de Crillon was a charter member.

More recently, the Dyers, father and son, bowing, were members, although under the tacit condition that they were always to arrive by the servants' entrance. Fräulein Whatever, of the steamer *Priscilla,* out of New York bound for Fall River, bombed, perhaps, some years later in Essen *(Now they can be proud again, the young men),* was a member, as a thousand nonmembers died or escaped dying once more in the shot-up planes above her head. Olson, caressing himself, running

for help when he should have been in twenty feet
of cold mountain water, was a member, accepted
the same day as Morris Kahn, who paid his dues
for a lifetime by driving the long way around a lake
in an ambulance with a dead fool on the stretcher
behind him. Mrs. Carol-Ann Humes, in her la-
mentable green dress, a little tipsy to drown her
timidity in this high company, sensitive of nose
and not ashamed to say that Pope John XXIII was
a Communist, was a member. Craven, the quarterback with the cocky street-fighter's face and the
naked greed for applause, stopped three times
within the two-yard line, was a member. *Fuck you,
brother.* The girl in the white dress on the eve of
the new year of 1933, having paid an unusually
high initiation fee, was a member. The beauty
with the loose shoulder strap was on the governing
committee and passed on all newcomers. The old
Irishwoman (*Scum,* she said), while given to
drink, was a member, although she knew her place
as she knew everybody's place. Louis's wife (*The
house in town, the place in Falmouth,* and *the pictures* and *the books—my blood, my balls, the marrow of my bones*) was a member. The lawyer
Rosenthal, ready to work on Sunday, or Yom Kippur, or on the matinée of the Second Coming of
the Lord, was a member. The croquet players on
the Belgian lawn were members. Leah Levinson
Ross Stafford had applied for membership, but
perhaps, despite her beauty, her application would
be tabled for further consideration. The high
school boys and girls in Dallas (*Kennedy gawn,*

Johnson next; Kennedy gawn, Johnson next) were all members.

The wind was dying down. An evening hush was settling over land and ocean. Gulls rose before him and sailed briefly out toward Hispaniola as he approached them. He walked with his head down, accompanied by the dead. It is only with the greatest care that memory can be kept from becoming a prison or a gallows.

Voices speak, faces appear, moments and images come and go—a promise broken, a false smile, a grave, a wedding night, a helmet in the rain, a father dancing, a son using the word "conspicuous," a vermouth stain on a pink dress, a lipstick stain on a sheet, the mouths of malice, the whispers of betrayal; all movements dangerous, equivocal; weapons everywhere, but targets concealed, the terms of victory or surrender never quite stated.

It sometimes takes more honor to walk the last hundred yards to your front door than to advance against the walls of a fortress.

How gratifying, how simple it is to go to the water's edge, continue . . . accomplish that one certain act to write finish to so many uncertain accomplishments.

He shivered. The Atlantic touched him with the first chill of evening, reminding him that glaciers fed these waters. He raised his head. Walking toward him was the blond girl with the two cats. The girl had wound her hair around her head in a crown. Was that all she had done that afternoon?

251

While the guns had sounded, during the hot hours when the sirens had wailed, the murders had been committed, the famous men had broadcast their lies; while the crowds had formed and fled, leaving their wounded on the cobblestones, had she just braided her hair under a dune, sheltered from the wind, with the two cats at her ankles?

She was close enough now for him to see her face. She was young and lovely, a Northern gift to the new continent, a wide clear brow under the weight of pale hair, wide clear eyes, summer-colored skin, the perfect, full, long body sculptured into a hieroglyph by the severe black suit, Miss America, Miss Universe, Miss Rose Bowl, Miss Aphrodite, Miss Pithecanthropus Erectus, with her golden crown.

Their eyes met for a moment. The girl did not smile, nor did he. It was not necessary. All that was necessary was that she was alive, that she was there, glittering and tall, a young animal of his own species, moving in grace, at home between sea and land, with her attendant beasts, sanctifying with their linked flesh the end of a summer's day.

He did not look behind him as she passed him, the cats now leading her along the small hiss of the ebbing tide.

The sun was nearly down. He approached his house. There were lights on in the kitchen, that pure small flame in the last of the daylight, more like a jewel than a source of illumination against the bright early-evening sky.

His wife and daughter were working in the

kitchen. They didn't see him as he looked in through the window. Their heads were bent as they went about their tasks, the lovely grave face of his wife, the brown dear promise of the face of his daughter. Their hair shone in the kitchen light. They had gone through the ceremony of beauty, the two women of the family, for the homecoming of the husband and father.

He looked through the window. His wife saw him. She smiled.

There are harbors left.

He went in through the kitchen door. He kissed his wife, smelled the clean hair, kissed his daughter, smelled the clean hair.

"What did you do all afternoon?" his wife asked.

"I watched a ball game," he said.

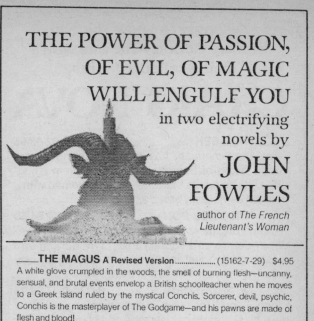